I0542152

Top of the Leader Board

ACE AND KITTY

BA TORTUGA

Ace and Kitty
ISBN # 978-1-78430-922-0
©Copyright BA Tortuga 2015
Cover Art by Posh Gosh ©Copyright December 2015
Interior text design by Claire Siemaszkiewicz
Totally Bound Publishing

ACE AND KITTY

Dedication

To my wife. You are my One True North.

Chapter One

Not one of the cowboys who saw him as the face of a major bull riding league would believe it, but Ace Porter hated celebrity-filled network parties with the fiery burning heat of a thousand suns. He hated the glitter and the fake smiles and the fact that he was the only one not wearing a suit.

Of course, he hated the suits more. They didn't go with his cowboy hat or scars.

He stuck one hand into the back pocket of his jeans, the other holding the beer he'd wheedled out of the bartender. It wasn't Bud Light, but it would do. The entire fucking room was filled with fake shit.

Fake smiles. Fake boobies. Fake hair.

Hell, there were probably fake backsides, built just for kissing.

That idea made him smile, which was a decent thing, because that meant he wasn't scowling when she came into view. Hoo yeah.

Blonde and lean, without a bit of fake anything showing, the lady moved as if those heels were the most natural things ever. Her hair was piled high, caught with a sparkly deal that caught the light, just like the jewels at her throat and ears. Damn, she was like a firefly or something—all shine and twinkle. Her dress was simple, dark and classy, showing leg, not too much chest, and he took a step closer.

Their gazes met, hooked on each other across the room, and she smiled back at him, eyes actually crinkling at the corners a little.

Crinkling.

Damn.

He hadn't seen a woman in this town whose face could still move. Ace straightened up, figuring he'd make his way over, see if she wanted to have a drink. Maybe compare wrinkles.

Or even better, compare scars.

Bright blue eyes looked him up and down, giving him as much of a once-over as he'd given her. Whatever she saw in him must have worked, because Ace got another of those approving smiles, then she raised her wineglass—filled with white—and nodded, right before a suit came up, took her elbow, and she rolled her eyes.

Damn. He circled like a shark, trying to be less than obvious. He figured for him he did okay. It was hard not to stand out in Wranglers and a Stetson. She was a stand-out, too, the black slip of a dress clinging where it ought to, and her sheer stockings had a line down the back, just the barest bit off-center. How erotic was that?

There was nothing plastic about her, and Ace shifted from foot to foot, getting a little growly at the guy who monopolized her time.

Those pretty eyes kept returning to him, over and over, and once he could swear he saw her mouth make the words, "*Save me.*"

Well, now. He was a cowboy, right? He couldn't deny a damsel in distress. Ace wandered on over, stepping neatly between the man and his prey. "Hey, there. Oh, sorry, man. You mind if I steal the lady for a moment? We were talking earlier and we got interrupted. Didn't want to miss the rest of that story."

Before the stuffed suit could reply, Ace had taken the lady's arm and swept her right off past a group of ladies who might have been from Dallas, the way their hair was jacked to Jesus. One of them caught the suit's arm when he tried to pursue. Boom. Day saved.

"Oh, you're very good." Her laugh was warm, not tittery or anything, just as right as rain. "Thank you. I was getting incredibly frustrated."

"You looked like it." He'd been pretty frustrated, too. "Ace."

"Kitty." Her hand was slender, long and warm, nails normal, not like claws or studded with diamonds or nothing. "Can I buy you another beer?"

"You can. You have to threaten someone to get it, though." He'd been there. If it was martinis or white wine, you were safe, but God forbid you ask for a cold brew.

"Not if we find another bar."

Well, hello there. Wasn't that refreshing candor, and initiative, as well? Ace approved.

"You as bored as I am?" He took her glass and put it on the tray of a passing waiter along with his beer bottle. "I know a great hole in the wall with a mechanical bull."

"Honestly?" Her eyes lit up like jewels and shit — he'd always thought that image was some made up deal, but hers were amazing. Genuinely. "I'm so in."

"Come on, then. You got a coat?"

It wasn't cold or nothin', but some of the LA types liked to have a fancy cover-up, and you had to stand

and wait for an hour while the coat check feller hunted it down.

"I don't." Kitty grinned, winked. "I have everything a girl needs right here." She patted the shiny leather purse on her shoulder.

"Well, come on, then, before someone else stops us." He grinned too, feeling like a young cowboy at his first big show — part excited, part nervous. Mostly tickled as a pig in shit.

"Do you have a car here?" She headed for the elevator, pressing the 'down' button.

"I do. You need to move yours or anything?" He stood close enough to smell her light, citrus-flavored perfume, but not close enough to be stalkery.

"Nope. I'm cabbing it. I'm not a local."

"Me either. Had to be out this way for an event anyway, though." More than one of the other league officials had accused him of being a control freak, not letting a show go on without his approval.

"How did I guess that you weren't from here?" She smiled, the words teasing, but not holding a hint of bitch in them.

"Oh, I don't know. Must be psychic." He winked. His Texas was hard to miss, from his accent to his boots, which were actually worn in.

She let her eyes go wide. "You know my secret! Everyone else here believes that you're a surfer from Venice Beach."

He laughed out loud, glad they were in the elevator because it would have drawn stares. "There you go. And you're a hick from Oklahoma who can't drive in cities to save you..."

"Absolutely. Possibly Arkansas. You never know."

He gave her face a careful once-over. "Nah. Too many teeth."

He put a hand on the small of her back to guide her toward the parking garage. He didn't quite trust them valets. The flashing lights and screaming from the paparazzi wasn't down here, either. Just a security guard. A great big one. A great big giant one that stood and loomed.

"Mr. Porter. Miss Carpenter. Is everything okay?" the guard asked.

Kitty flashed the man a smile. "Just fine. We're heading out."

"Have a good evening, ma'am."

Ace waited until they got into the truck. "LA security is always sort of robotic."

"They only hire Teamsters in the city."

Huh. New York. She didn't sound like New York. She didn't act like New York.

"So, where are you from originally?" Ace liked that she had that newscaster voice, really. Smooth and accentless.

"Missouri, right outside of Kansas City. You're from Texas, yes?"

"I am. I have a place down by Weatherford now, but I'm from West Texas." Small town, deep West Texas.

"I've been in Texas a few times. It's a vast place. Missouri, not as much."

"It's big, yeah." He steered away from the big hotels and convention areas, heading for the seedier bars.

It said something to him, that she didn't tense up, didn't ask where they were going. Hopefully it didn't say she was stupid.

The bar was damned near a half-hour away and by the time they'd parked, he'd learned that she'd had a Chihuahua for years that had only recently died, that she liked hot wings and that her laugh was less like tinkling bells and more like a full-on gut burst.

He'd told her about his momma's fascination with them naked hairless cats, about the horrors of working on a septic tank and about his Charley—the grumpy, raw-boned bastard that he loved to ride above all the other horses in the stables.

"How do you feel about fried onions?" Ace loved the toothpick thingees at this bar.

"I think that fried food is a sign that there is a God and he loves us, no matter what the surgeon general says about it."

"Then you're the girl for me to bring here." He took her hand to help her out of the truck. Her heels might be treacherous on the uneven pavement.

"Thank you." She let him help her inside without a fuss, even grinning when the bouncer—who seemed twelve if he was a day—hopped up, obviously recognizing Ace.

"Mr. Porter, sir. Good to see you."

Ace nodded, grinned, secretly pleased as punch. "Still got that mechanical bull, son?"

"Yes, sir. We surely do. Come on in. It's real quiet tonight. So good to see you again."

"Thanks." He shook the kid's hand since he couldn't remember ever seeing him before and had no name to use.

Kitty chuckled, followed him in. "You've been here before."

"Few times, yeah." The kid at the door had the look of a transplanted rodeo fan, anyway. Someone who would know him no matter where he was. The kid was right, the bar was quiet, peaceful, and Ace found them a little booth in the back.

"This okay?" He wanted it to be private enough for them to talk.

"This is just fine, thank you." Kitty put her purse down beside her on the table, her little silvery watch clicking on the wood.

"You want a beer? I think they might have something decent here." Hell, they might even have Shiner.

"Sure. Decent beer is infinitely preferable to the watered-down grape juice they were calling wine." Kitty had the prettiest smile — it lit her whole face up.

"I like your style, lady." He waved the little waitress over, ignoring the fake tits she presented in her low-cut Daisy Duke knock-off outfit. "You still have Shiner here, hon?"

"We sure do, honey. Y'all need menus?" Her accent was so fake it made his teeth itch.

"Yes, please." Ace waited for the girl to sashay off before grinning a little at Kitty. "You're not an actress, right?"

"God, no. I can't act my way out of a paper bag." That laugh rang out again, warm and purely tickled. "I'm a news reporter."

Something stirred in the back of his mind and Ace felt his cheeks heat. "Lord, I ought to know who you are, huh?"

"Well, given that you have a poster prominently displayed here and I don't know you, let's call it even, huh?" She touched his wrist. "Sometimes it's good to get to know somebody from the start."

"Yeah." His skin heated right up under her touch. "So, I'm a bull rider, and you're a reporter. Do you eat meat?" Wait, he knew that. Well, she ate chicken. "Steak, I mean."

"I am an omnivore, honestly. I have to be, for work. You wouldn't believe the weirdness people pretend to enjoy just to shock a girl."

"I promise never to pretend I like calf fries." Ace shuddered. "A guy like me can't kiss a vegetarian girl."

That laugh happened again, and her carefully arranged hair started to fall a little, blonde curls framing her face. "No. I don't imagine so. You've got beef sunk into your skin."

"Something like that." He couldn't hack it — he had to turn and look over his shoulder to see what poster she was talking about. Oh, jeez, he'd been young then. Him and Lucky and Cash and Steele all had. The Four Horsemen. God, they'd played hard. He missed it. Not all the time, of course, but enough. They'd had more fun than was reasonable.

"Oh, man. I smell a story."

"Huh?" He blinked, then laughed. "More like a thousand stories, and all bad."

Kitty chuckled. "Not all bad. I can tell that from the poster alone. That sort of connection can't be faked. I bet you four got into scrapes. Do you still ride?"

"Only in the exhibitions. I'm all corporate now." Someone had to keep the suits from taking it too far, and he sure couldn't see Steele or Baltazar Silva doing it.

"You're a suit? How fun is that?" Her toe nudged his calf, barely brushing it. "I am, most definitely, not a suit. The network biggies hate me."

"Oh, me, too." Sandy was a decent guy, but they had an uneasy truce at best.

"So what were you doing at Mandy's party? Are you looking or being looked at?"

"Both, I reckon. We're trying to get one of the big satellite networks to carry our events. What about you? Why were you schmoozing?" The beer and menus came, and he was glad to see she wasn't a delicate sipper.

"There's a journalist here in LA with connections to someone I'm interested in talking to in Chihuahua. I was hoping to corner him, but he didn't show. I did talk to his housekeeper, though, and I know where he's going to be in two days." Her eyes were sharp suddenly, and her nose twitched. God, that was hot. A hunter on the trail of prey.

"You got a way in, huh?" Two days. That could be promising if she needed to stick around.

"That's all I need. Of course, now I have to cool my heels."

"Oh, I'm sure you can think of something to do." Ace could. He could think of lots.

That smile was knowing, wicked, a little naughty, and it made him go zing. "I'm a smart lady."

"I bet you are." Ace paused, glancing at the menu. "If we both eat the onions, there won't be an issue, huh?"

"You are a smart man, but before we get into that, I have to ask. Are you involved with someone? I'm not opposed to having a little fun, but I've been the one who got cheated on more than once. I'm not interested in that."

"No, ma'am. My last long-time thing was when I was still riding with them." He jerked a thumb over his shoulder at the Four Horsemen, hoping that didn't make him sound too desperate.

"Mine was long enough ago that he's married to a soap opera diva and has two babies, so we're fair." She leaned back. "Besides, it takes a strong man to get past Leroy."

"Leroy?" He frowned a little. "I thought you said you weren't involved?"

Kitty held up one finger in the universal 'hold on' gesture, dug in her purse, pulled out a little phone and started pushing buttons before showing him the picture of a huge older man, shoulders four times as wide as his, holding a tiny baby in his big, dark hands. "This is Leroy and his new daughter. He's my cameraman, my best friend. He's my hero."

"Ah." Well, that was better. He nodded. "The one on the end on the right? That's my best buddy Steele Flanagan."

"That's a great name." She wiggled a little and Ace heard the heels click as they fell on the floor and she tucked her feet under her.

"Yeah. I tease him unmercifully." They shared a grin that was all about best friends.

They ordered onion rings and hot wings and another round of Shiner. Every time she laughed, more curls got loose from her bun, surrounding her face. She was fascinating. She was real. Ace was a little worried, because a guy like him could get to needing a lady like her.

The music started playing, the lights went down, and she touched his wrist again, fingertips warm and soft. "So you travel most of the time?"

"I'm on the road a good bit, yeah. We do about three months off a year." He turned his hand, his fingers gripping hers lightly.

"I'm more random than that. I can be off on assignment for months sometimes. Honey wants to kill us."

"Honey?" He was feeling a little like he'd been dropped in a weird TV show or something.

"Sorry. Leroy's wife. She's a force of nature."

"Ah. Sorry. Most of my friends aren't married." Okay, how stupid was that to say? Way to announce that cowboys could have trouble settling down.

"Most of your friends are young, hot cowboys, I bet." Kitty's cheeks were pinking, too.

"Shit. We ain't that young." This was getting ridiculous. George Strait came on the sound system and Ace stood. "You dance?"

"If you can lead, I can follow." She slipped the heels back on, then took his hand.

"I'm not bad." He was no Andy Baxter, who could dance a lady right out of her shoes, but he could cut a rug. He pulled Kitty close and got the rhythm in his head before two-stepping her around the floor.

The lady was about as lean as Jason Scott — damn near bird-like in his arms — and he worried about hurting her just by holding her. Kitty didn't seem to worry about that at all, proving she could follow along, easy as pie. She smelled right, like honey and citrus and a hint of musk.

They took a moment or two to really get settled, but suddenly he wound his arm around her waist, and his other hand held hers, and her hips were lined up in the cradle of his, her feet moving like they were attached to the toes of his boots. She relaxed in his arms — as if she did this every day, leaned into the swing of it and trusted him to move her around. He kind of hoped she didn't do it every day, though, as this was the first time she'd done it with him.

They two-stepped to three songs, then the music slowed, turning to a belt-buckle polisher.

Ace held her close, noticing that their food hadn't come. Then he rested his cheek on her head, keeping his hat right out of the way.

"You smell like heaven." She felt fine as frog hair against him, soft and warm.

"Just Old Spice." Some big old fragrance company had offered him his own smell-good, but he'd never been able to give up the white bottle.

"My dad used to wear that, when he was going out to dinner. It smells better on you."

"Thanks." She smelled fine, too, and felt amazing in his arms. She was stronger than she looked, not near as delicate. "You're a fine dancer, lady."

"Thank you. You make it easy."

The waitress put their food on the table, nodded at him, smiled.

Ace winked at the girl over Kitty's shoulder, but didn't end the dance until the song was over. He had ahold of the hottest thing he'd seen in years. Onions and wings could wait.

Chapter Two

Her feet hurt from dancing, her belly hurt from laughing and her lips were never going to recover from the nuclear-hot chicken wings. Kitty hadn't had so much fun since the prince of a tiny sovereignty in south Asia had tried to make her his eighth wife.

She shook her head as the waitress asked if she wanted another beer. "No. No, that was plenty."

No matter what happened, she wanted it to happen because she was into it, sober and aware.

Ace waved the girl off, too. "No, I got to drive, honey. Thanks, though."

"Are you interested in getting a cup of coffee, Ace?" Kitty wasn't ready for the night to end, not at all. She hadn't felt so relaxed with a man since she'd broken up with Jesse three years ago.

"I'd love to." He stood and offered her a hand, and she was pleased to see he not only paid the bill, but left a great tip for their waitress. She didn't need a man with money, but it was hard to respect a man who would screw a waitress out of her earnings.

She slid her fingers into his and they headed out, her feet screaming at her. The shoes were great for parties, but she hadn't intended to dance.

He helped her into his truck, frowning a little when she winced. "You all right?" She noticed he never called her honey or hon or whatever he'd called all the other girls all night.

"I'm fine. Been on these heels for a long time. Nothing worth worrying about. After all, I need all the inches I can get."

He blinked at her, then broke out laughing, which made her go back over her words. *Oops.* He was still chuckling when he slid into the driver's seat. "So, where to?"

"Well, I'm at the LAX Hilton. There's a coffee bar there. Or I can look on my phone, find a place." At the hotel, she could pop into her suite, dress down a little.

"The Hilton is fine." He gave her a sideways look. "I'm just at the big Sheraton. They have room service, and I have a hot tub suite. We could drop by and get a swimsuit for you."

"That sounds perfect." God, he was hot. How he'd managed to say something that would have been smarmy from any other man and make it gentlemanly, she didn't know.

"Cool." His dimples deepened, outlining the vicious scar beside his mouth, carved deeply in his cheek. "The hot tub will be great for your feet, too."

"Hot tubs are more proof that there's a God, you know." They pulled into the Hilton. "Do you want to wait for me? I'll be just a second."

Long enough to change, grab a toothbrush and some condoms from her toiletry bag, and her bikini.

"Sure. Why don't I get us a head start on the coffee down in the lobby?"

"That's a plan." She headed in, looking away from the random flash of camera, then slipped her shoes off in the elevator. On the way, she checked messages. Leroy. Four times.

She hit 'one' on speed dial, making her way toward her room. "Hey, Big Daddy. What's up?"

"Been trying to get ahold of you, Kit. Where the hell are you?"

"I met someone. He took me dancing." Someone strong and funny with these amazing smile lines.

"No shit?" Leroy's voice went all Big Daddy for real. "You be careful."

"I am. I swear. His name's Ace Porter. I'm going over to the Sheraton with him. He's with that sports club — the cowboy one."

"Huh. I'll Google him. Keep your damned phone on for a little bit." Oh, growly.

"I promise. He's not skeezy." Not at all.

"Well, you'll have to forgive me if I don't trust your taste one hundred percent." Now he was harping on an old joke between them.

"Crusty old bastard." She smiled at the phone. "Don't you have a wife to let yell at you?"

"Yeah, yeah. I'll call in a few." Leroy made some disgusting kissy noises and hung up.

It only took her a couple of seconds to change into her bikini, throw a pair of jeans and a T-shirt over the top of it and pull her hair into a ponytail. A pair of sandals on her feet, a pair of clean panties in her purse along with a few rubbers, and she was ready to go.

Ace waited for her downstairs, two cardboard cups in hand, and it occurred to her that he'd never asked her what she wanted. "I got you one of them Americano things with a shot of vanilla. Is that okay?"

"That's perfect." She grinned at him, tickled. She didn't mind frou-frou coffee, but she'd cut her teeth on black newsroom Joe.

"Cool." When he had a free hand he wrapped it around her waist and guided her out. "I think I like this look better than the dress and heels, for sure."

"It's infinitely more comfortable." She bumped hips with him. "That's why I'm not trying to be an anchor. Well, that and I love my job. It's always new."

"So you're like a roving reporter, huh?" His hip bumped hers right back, his hand lingering on the small of her back, his fingers warm through the thin cotton of her T-shirt.

"Sort of. I cover foreign affairs, mostly. I've been to Iraq, Somalia, Guatemala. Mexico is my beat now." She knew it hadn't started because she was a great journalist. She'd gotten her foot in the door because she was little and pretty and blonde and the head of the MRO in Columbia had a thing for tiny blondes.

She'd kept her job because she was a fabulous fucking journalist.

"Wow. Worst I ever get is Sao Paulo."

"That's a harsh city, if you're on your own. But the people are fascinating." And the food was fab.

"It's a good city for rodeo. They love their bull riding." The drive to the Sheraton took maybe five minutes.

The coffee was strong and sweet, waking her right up. "And their plastic surgery."

"Lord. We got one bull rider from there who does, like, a thousand crunches a day." Ace grinned over. "You don't seem like the surgery type."

"Ace. No one on earth gets plastic surgery to have boobs like mine." She knew full well that she was…less than endowed.

"Yeah, but you don't have that scary surprised face and weird swollen lips." Ace parked far enough out that she was glad she'd ditched the heels. "'Sides, I like your boobs just fine."

She grinned over at him, twirled once. "Me and the girls thank you and your tight little tush."

His cheeks pinked a bit, but he didn't seem put out, really. More pleased. He swept her through the lobby and right into an elevator. No drama. No worries. No hesitation. She loved it. The room was no penthouse suite or anything, but it was neat and comfortable and the hot tub took center stage. Woo.

She put her purse on the chair by the door, then headed to the window to look out at the lights, to give Ace a chance to settle.

"Be right back, darlin'." He disappeared into the bathroom, taking something out of his suitcase. She wondered if darlin' was one step up from honey. She hoped for more than one step.

"You want me to get the bubbles going?"

"Sure!" She heard boots thudding on the tiles, and heard him whistling some country-sounding song.

Kitty stripped down to her bikini, then started the heat and bubbles on the dial before slipping into the tub. Oh, that was nice. The man had exceptional taste in hotels. He had decent taste in bathing suits, too. Not too baggy, not too tight. Not too long. He was compact, but ripped, with a belly that you could play like a marimba.

She caught herself licking her lips. "Hey, there."

"Hey." Ace came to the edge of the tub and looked down. "Sorry I missed the unveiling."

She chuckled, pulled herself up hip-high, the water pouring off her.

"Oh, better." Ace slipped into the tub next to her and pulled her down. "Damn. I should have gotten the room service menu.

"I'll get it in a minute." Their bodies slid and slipped together.

"Sounds like a plan." The water couldn't compete with the heat of his body. The promise of the Wranglers and starched shirt delivered completely once they were stripped off.

One of her legs floated over the top of his, the water carrying it, and his hand landed on her thigh, holding her there, a sweet, firm weight. Nothing intrusive.

Her hair started falling and she grabbed it, twisting the ponytail into a loose bun. It wasn't until she saw his eyes on her chest, her hard nipples pushing at the swimsuit top, that she realized how much that pose showed off her assets.

His fingers tightened on her leg then relaxed, stroking the tiny sting away. Ace cleared his throat. "Sorry."

"You're okay." She was floating. Her cheek rested on his shoulder. "This good?"

"This is as good as I can remember being."

Oh, that made her smile. It was the easiest thing she'd done, to look into the warmest hazel eyes she'd ever seen, and press their lips together.

Ace hummed a little and his free hand slid up around her back to her neck, just like when they'd gone two-stepping. His body pressed against one side of hers, his lean muscles shifting. Their lips moved together, the kiss sweet and slow. She touched his bottom lip with her tongue, traced the curve carefully.

His fingers pushed under the ponytail holder in her hair, tugging it loose. Good man, he didn't snag it. The wild mass came down and he moaned for her, pulled her closer. She floated farther into his lap, found herself straddling both of his slick, muscled thighs.

"Definitely like the bikini." He pushed up into her a little, and she could feel how much he liked.

His belly felt so right against hers, and her nipples ached where she rubbed against him.

Ace smiled, the bare hint of stubble tickling her mouth as he kissed her again and again. He wasn't in any kind of hurry, his hands traveling slowly on her skin as if he wanted to map every inch of her. They started moving together like they were dancing again, easy as breathing.

He still smelled perfect, even hot and wet. That was an excellent sign.

Her fingers found all sorts of scars — some heavy and ropy, some light and barely there. They fascinated her fingers. There was one on his elbow that seemed huge, like it had been catastrophic. She'd seen enough of violence to know that had hurt bad. She cupped his elbow, holding it, sort of being thankful it was healed, she guessed.

He made an inquiring sort of noise, his mouth running down her neck. He was curious, tasting every bit of her skin.

"Poor elbow…" She arched a little bit, chin lifting. *Oh, right there.*

"Why I retired." His words made her shiver, every puff of air making her moan. Between the hot water, the cool air and that breath, she was going to melt into a pile of goo. Or a puddle. A pile was tough to accomplish in the hot tub.

She almost laughed at herself, but he eased her up a little farther out of the bubbles, lips finding one of her nipples through the bikini top.

That stopped all her laughter.

"Can we get rid of this thing?" He plucked at the tie at the back of the top.

"We so can." She reached back, undid the middle tie then the one at the neck, the bits of black material dropping into the water.

"Better." He lifted her a little higher, his arm muscles bulging, and licked her nipple, then sucked.

"Ace." Her belly went tight and she surged forward, the warm arousal getting sharp, turning into need.

His thigh floated up, pressing between hers, spreading her wider. Her teeth sank into her bottom lip, the pressure of his leg close to perfect. She rocked a little, moaning as he nudged her clit and sent a deep ache slamming through her.

Ace huffed out a hard breath, his body slipping under hers, his cock pushing against the thin swim shorts. "More, darlin'."

"Yes." She scooted closer, eyes rolling as she slipped against his cock, letting herself feel the promise in that hard length.

"Uhn." He made a great noise, all man and a lot redneck. His hand worked under her ass, pushing her in a rhythm that made her eyes cross.

"Fuck. I want…" Kitty wanted to feel him long and hot inside her. She slammed their mouths together, sliding faster.

Ace grunted and her string bikini bottom went flying, landing with a sodden plop on the floor. His fingers slid between her legs, rubbing at her. Kitty cried out into Ace's lips as heat flooded her. His fingers were sure, the touch just right, circling and sliding over her clit. This cowboy knew what he wanted, and he took it. Damn, she liked that in a man. Her body moved as if she had no control over it, bucking and rolling as his fingers made her gasp. He knew how to touch. Not too hard, not too soft, he rubbed her little nub over and over, the tiny circles making her hips rock and roll.

The pressure built and she couldn't catch her breath. She knew she should touch him, make him feel as good as she was, but she was trapped, caught in the pleasure.

Ace didn't seem to care a bit. He watched her with those pretty hazel eyes and moved her up and down and around and around until she wanted to scream. Her head fell back as she came, her thighs shaking, her body feeling as if it was burning up.

"So pretty." He murmured it against her throat, his lips so hot, brushing back and forth.

"So fine." She shivered, her nipples hard as nails. "God, you feel good."

"There's more to feel, darlin'." He took her hand, pushing it down against his swim shorts.

"Plenty to feel." She measured him, base to tip, through the wet fabric, then she set to untying the waist. She wanted skin. The knot fought her for a moment, but soon enough it gave under her touch and she pulled the wet fabric off him. She used one finger to trace his length, circling around the ridge at the tip with her nail, and he groaned for her, his body rocking under hers hard enough that water splashed. Oh, he liked that. She licked her lips as she let her finger nudge the slit. They needed a bed. Having him underwater was inconvenient as hell.

"We—" He stopped to pant a moment, his head down on her shoulder. "We ought to go to bed, darlin'."

"God, yes." *Mind reader*. She nodded, stroked one more time. "I want you."

"Yeah. Oh, God, yeah. I may even have a condom." He gave her this crazy grin, his dimples digging deep in his cheeks. Then he kind of…lifted them out of the tub as if it wasn't slick and scary.

"If you don't, I put some in my purse back at the hotel." She held on, a little breathless. Strong. How could somebody be so strong?

"Smart girl. I like that." He laughed, and they dripped all the way to the bed.

"Always be prepared." She chuckled as he lowered her to the mattress.

"It's a good motto." His wet shorts went down with a plop.

"Fabulous." She let one foot trail along his leg, eyes eating him up. Compact and firm, solid and hard—he made her mouth water. His belly sucked in with a sharp breath, and Ace laughed before pressing down on top of her.

They fit together, hand in glove, and she rocked up, sliding on his cock, knowing her wet curls had to feel almost as fine as the pressure to her clit.

"Uhn." His hands clenched on her ass and it felt even better without the water. They were making their own heat. Who needed bubbles?

"Yes." She did it again, then one more time, biting her lip against the yell that wanted out.

"Kiss me, darlin'." He drew her down, lips sealing hers. They started moving together, finding a rocking, sliding rhythm, their lower bodies riding. His cock felt hot, not huge but nice and hard and perfect for her. He finally grabbed her hips to stop her, though, his chest heaving. "Rubber."

"You got it. My purse is right there in the chair."

"Got it." He snagged her purse, cussing about how everything in there was black on a black liner. It was a universal boy complaint.

Kitty grinned. "Hand it over."

She pulled out the little packet with a "Ta da!"

"Come on, darlin'. I'm teetering." He grinned, his hands seeming to automatically head for her breasts.

"Teeter, teet—" Her tease lost itself as his fingers found her nipples, the little tug going right to her clit. "Oh…"

"Do not mock, darlin'." He grinned. "Come on."

"Right. Do that again and I'll be in trouble." She got a little crinkly square out, opening it.

"Yeah?" He did it again.

She dropped the condom, arched. "Ace!"

"Well, shit, darlin'." He sounded so happy that it didn't come across as scolding. He picked it up with his free hand. "Try again."

"Sorry." She maintained that girls with smaller breasts had more sensitive nipples, every time. She grabbed the rubber, got it out of the package this time.

Ace waited, his fingers poised to have another go at her. Such a boy.

"You be good, now." She started to laugh.

"What fun is being good when there's hot sex to be had?"

That made her laugh, and she managed to get the condom slid halfway down Ace's cock. He finally helped her out, his hand joining hers and pushing the latex down.

Her eyelids got heavy and she found his balls with her fingers, rolling them in their sac.

"Damn. Just…" Ace bucked for her, his hands coming up to catch her breasts again.

"Ace." He pulled and tugged at her nipples, rolling enough that heat flooded her.

"You ready to ride, darlin'?" He pushed one more time, reminding her that his dick was right there.

"Y-yes. Yes, Ace. In." And she made a living talking. *Wow.*

"Yeah." His warm touch fell to her hips, lifting her. He positioned her easily, moving her into place. His fingers tested her wetness, slipping to tease her clit for a second, then he pushed inside, filling her. Her nails dug into his chest. Thank goodness she kept them short.

They found that rhythm right off, one of his hands on her hip keeping her right there, rubbing against him. They fit together a little like they were made for it. She felt him everywhere, better than dancing, his hip bones rocking into her, his balls swinging against her.

He touched her with the hand that wasn't guiding her motions, fingers slipping to her cheek then down the center of her chest.

"Good." God, she could feel every inch of him.

"I—yeah. Good." His eyes met hers and she shivered. The look was hot-hot. Better than good.

She reached out, stroked his lips. That made his hips jerk, and her eyes rolled.

"Oh, hell, darlin'." He was starting to shake, really close to the edge. His cock swelled inside her until the fit was impossibly tight.

"Close. Please." She wasn't above begging, really.

"Yeah." He heard, and better than that, he understood. He moved down to stroke between them, sliding against her right above where they came together.

That was all it took—one touch and she was crying out, coming for him.

"Oh, Lord..." His eyes finally let hers go, rolling back in his head. He came hard for her, every muscle in his body shaking. The pleasure kept going—on and on— and she watched him, admired him, the whole time.

She'd had lovers, but this... He was pure male.

There was nothing soft or slick or civilized about him. He fascinated her. Kitty let one hand slide down his belly, petting him all the way down. "Hot."

He chuckled, his abs going tight under her hand. "Feels fine as frog hair."

"Yeah." His musculature fascinated her fingers.

He grinned wider, his hands moving all over her, too. "Like what you see, huh?"

"I do, indeed. You?" She knew there were better-looking women, especially here in LA.

"Hell, yes. You're not all plastic." His thumb rubbed her nipple.

Her eyes crossed a little and her teeth sank into her bottom lip. "No. All natural."

She didn't have the kind of time to do the sort of recovery plastic surgery required. Maybe in a few years she'd buy herself a C-cup.

"Good. I like it." He proved it, too, playing with her breasts until she wanted to scream. Her breath was caught in her chest, and her clit felt like every move on Ace's cock was almost a touch. Her nipples ached, each little pull and tug and twist making that coil of heat in her belly tighter.

"Lord, darlin'. I— God." Tendons pulled in his neck, his grin turning to a grimace. She could feel him, hot and harder than she could have believed.

She nodded, hips rolling faster. "Please."

"Yeah. Yeah, darlin'." Ace curled into her and caught her nipple with his lips, sucking hard.

She cried out, fingers tangling in his hair as the rush of yet another orgasm started, slamming through her, the pleasure going on and on. Ace shook against her, his hands on her skin, his mouth against her breast. She could hear him making these amazing noises, primal as hell.

One climax melted into another, surprising her, leaving her shaking around his cock.

"Goddamn…" He breathed the word, a tiny puff of sound.

"Wow." She couldn't quite keep her head up.

"Yeah." Ace eased her down, giving her something to rest on to help keep her afloat. The whole world was spinning.

Her fingers explored him, moving lazily as she gathered her brain back together.

He held her, solid as a rock, even if his chest rose and fell a little hard. "I like your style, Kitty."

"I like your everything, Ace." She chuckled, kissed his chin. "This is where we have the taxi or breakfast discussion, hmm?"

She was rooting for breakfast. Possibly lunch, too. Nice, late dinner.

"I vote for breakfast."

Woo hoo.

"Excellent. I love a nice breakfast." Kitty winked, settled.

"Me, too. I like a little morning exercise." He put an arm around her, getting her right down against his shoulder.

"Running?" she teased. "Yoga? Pilates?"

"Huh. I was thinking horizontal aerobics."

"Like how you think." She was dozing off, his touch relaxing her, bone deep.

"Good. We'll make it a plan." His voice was getting muzzy.

Kitty liked a man with a plan.

Chapter Three

Ace woke in the morning feeling a little stiff, a little bruised and a lot happy. Hell, his phone hadn't rung all damned night and he had a warm, beautiful woman next to him.

All of a sudden life was good.

God, she was something—tiny and blonde, with a little pointed chin and a full mouth. Her hand was on his belly. She wasn't curvy, but even as small as she was, she wasn't dainty. She could power through hot wings and burp like a sailor, and she could ride like a rodeo cowboy who was broke and desperate. Her skin was soft as goose feathers, though, and her hair was heavy and sweet and curled around his fingers.

"Warm." One of her feet slipped along his leg, caressing him.

It was like something out of a movie. Surely nothing like anything he'd had in years. God, it felt right. "Morning."

"Morning." She grinned at him, her mascara all smudged, giving her smoky eyes.

"You sleep okay?" He had. Like a rock.

"I did. You?" Her hand slid down his side, petting him.

"I'm surprised I didn't snore." Maybe he had because God knew Steele had always accused him of it when they were on the road. She didn't seem bothered.

She found his hip, fingertips circling it lazily. "If you did, it didn't wake me."

His skin started to tingle, almost ache. Ace drew in a deep breath, trying to settle a little. "Well, that's good. You didn't cause me any stress, either."

Her cheek rested on his shoulder again, her hand still moving, exploring him. His belly muscles quivered the barest bit, his hips moving restlessly. He eased his hand down to rest on her ass.

"This okay?" Her fingers were in his pubes now, tickling the edges.

"Uh— Yeah. Yeah. That's just fine." *Better than fine. Amazing.*

"Excellent." Jesus, she was…thorough. She rolled his balls, thumbnail barely scraping the join of leg and body.

He jerked like he'd been stung, his cock rising harder and faster. Lord. "You—oh." He lost his breath, his speech.

"Mmhmm." Little sex kitten. She moved against him, rocking sweet and slow against his thigh even as she started to draw a line up and down his cock.

Ace dug his heels into the mattress and he lifted to let her touch some more. He liked letting her get the lay of the land, letting her lead for the time being.

She traced one nipple to aching hardness, then she started to explore his ribs.

"Teasing." He vibrated, fighting the urge to roll her beneath him and ride. *Goddamn.*

"No. No, exploring, not teasing." Her lips joined in the mapping, one hand at his balls again while she nibbled the scar along his shoulder.

"I like it." He did. A lot. His cock was slapping against his belly, he liked it so much.

"I do, too." *Oh, fuck a duck sideways*, she was heading south with those pretty lips, even as her fingers circled his shaft. He knew what came next, and he watched her as though he was watching the elusive decent porn movie.

"A little lower, darlin'." He grinned, driving up again. He was a greedy man.

"Hmm? Here?" His sweet lady nibbled his nipple as she teased his thigh.

"That's nice, but that's not it." He reached down to move her hand over a bit. Her laugh tickled his ribs and her touch felt right enough that his toes curled. "Oh, yeah." Shit, he was gonna bust before she got to doing anything serious.

"You smell good. Did I mention that?" She headed south faster, lips on his belly now, her hair slick and cool around the base of his cock.

"You might have, but feel free to say it again." He eased one hand into her hair, feeling the weight of it, the silkiness, the way it clung. The tip of her tongue brushed his cock, made his toes curl again right before she took him into that wild, sucking heat. Ace almost shouted, his body trying to roll up around her. He held off by sheer will. His eyes felt like they were burning in his skull. Most girls a man had to nudge real hard into sucking, but this one… *Damn*.

She liked it. He could tell. It was happy-making in a huge way, how much she was enjoying herself.

Her lips squeezed, dragging up and down around him. The pressure built in his balls, her every motion enticing more sounds out of him.

"Oh, darlin'. Damn. Kitty." Her name spilled out over and over while he got himself an eyeful of that sweet little ass, the pretty blonde curls peeking out between her legs. He could smell her, too, sweet and tart, and he wanted him a taste.

"Mmhmm…" His balls got a tug, a little nudge. *Jesus. Girl.*

Moaning, Ace rode each touch, bucking like a futurity bull, all but thrashing for her. She was like fire. He didn't hardly have time to warn her that he was coming, but she didn't back away from him, didn't tease. Jesus, she was something.

Ace panted, his hand still tangled in her hair. Man, he was going to have to do something special to pay her back for that. A woman needed to know how damned special a man thought she was, after all, no matter what she did.

She kissed the tip of his cock, then his belly. "Morning."

"Hey." Ace smiled down when she glanced up. "That was a fine howdy."

"It seemed like a good idea." Damn, she had a wicked twinkle in her eyes, the blue like a clear summer morning in Colorado or Wyoming.

"I liked it, for sure. I might even order waffles for that." He tugged at her shoulder with his free hand, wanting her pressed to him again.

"With strawberries and whipped cream?" She slid back up his body.

"Oh, that's an idea. Long as that's what you want." He could see the advantages of berries and cream and her skin.

"I do. Sweet and smooth and decadent." She settled beside him like she belonged there and he slid his fingers along her thigh, wanting proof that she was as into this as he was. Her folds were hot, slick and wet, ready for him. He petted her sweet lips, watching her face go a little slack.

Somebody needed him, too. Badly.

"You got the cream I need, darlin'." He rolled over on top of her, fingertip flicking her clit even as he stole an almost chaste kiss. "Want a taste of you."

"Oh, God." She closed her eyes, swallowing hard enough that Ace saw her throat work.

He'd take that as a yes.

He slipped down, lips stopping to tug one of those tight, hard little nipples. She was sensitive there, and he already loved knowing that she needed that play to start her engine. Start it it did, too. She cried right out, the wetness around his fingers flowing all that much more.

He let his tongue linger over the bud, flick it against his teeth, and her hands landed on his head. *Hell, yes.*

Ace figured he could stay right there, but there was that sweet pussy to explore, and he wanted to taste, needed to feel her come again. He let go of her nipple reluctantly, not wasting any time as he scooted down, chin nudging her curls.

"Oh. Oh, Ace. Please, huh?"

"Yeah, darlin'. I got you." He spread her some, thumbs sliding on her pretty pink lips so he could drag his tongue along her, gathering her flavor. Sweet. Damn, she was sweet and tart, and he wanted more.

He circled her swollen clit with his tongue and Kitty rolled into his hands, her ass firm and round and perfect. He traced around that needy bit of flesh twice more, then wrapped his lips around it and sucked, lashing with his tongue at the same time.

"Ace!" Kitty almost sat up, driving into him, and he grinned as best he could. *Hell, yeah. Just like that, darlin'. Give it up for me.*

He alternated between sucking and licking, between a light, teasing touch and gifting her everything he had.

Kitty gave it right up for him, twisting and moaning, rocking like she was riding. Her soft cries got louder, more desperate, and he slipped down, reaching for her hard nipples as he fucked her with his tongue. As soon as he got his fingers around those nips she arched, head lifting as she drove down, her cunt fluttering around him.

Hell, yes.

He kept licking all through her orgasm, loving on her, tasting how pleasure made her sweeter, more mellow.

"Oh, damn. I. Ace. Wow."

Chuckling, he kissed the soft curve under her bellybutton then along her ribcage. "Good for you, darlin'."

She snorted. "Nope. It sucked. You should try again, later."

That cracked his shit up and he cackled as he settled, pulling her into the curve of his body. His arm went around her, natural and right, and Ace hummed a bit. They had plenty of time to order breakfast.

Hell, if he was lucky, he'd get breakfast, lunch, then con her into dinner.

A man could dream, couldn't he?

Chapter Four

"Ace, have you seen my bikini bottoms?" They'd spent two glorious days together, laughing and eating decadent food and not answering either of their phones. Then her contact about the Mexico story had called. Damn it all, she hated when reality intruded on a sweet dream.

"Check in that laundry we sent out."

She laughed, digging in the closet for the plastic bag, thinking how they'd argued over whose expense account that was going on. In the end, Ace had given in gracefully because he'd covered all the meals. Including the biggest slice of carrot cake she'd ever seen.

Then they'd had to have housekeeping come in and change the sheets.

"What are you laughing about, darlin'?" Ace asked, his hands sliding on her butt, massaging her surprisingly sore muscles.

"Never eat carrot cake in bed. Ah-ha!" She pulled out her clothes before backing out of the closet, colliding with his solid body.

She hummed, his warmth something she was going to miss.

Ace chuckled, the sound low and intimate, sending shivers down her spine. "Too true. Those pineapple chunks can really burn."

"I have to get back to work, Ace. So do you. I wish I could stay one more day."

"Or week." He sighed, then kissed the nape of her neck before moving away. "Is this where we give over our phone numbers and say call me and walk away?"

"I'm better at email." She turned, gave her best on camera grin.

Ace grimaced. "Don't do that to me, darlin'. Just promise me you had the best damned weekend of your life. The rest may or may not happen, no matter how determined I am to see you again, but that I would believe."

She walked over to put her hands on his chest, tilting her chin up. Ace gave her the kiss she wanted, slow and thorough and perfect all the way to her toes. "Definitely the most amazing weekend of my life, Ace. I solemnly swear."

"Good deal." Those eye lines crinkled up and his dimples popped out. "I like you an awful lot, Kitty. Holler at me when you can."

"I will. Do you happen to have sunglasses I can borrow?" She'd come to his hotel at night, not even thinking about leaving in the harsh light of day.

"If you can pull off aviator shades they're yours." He winked for her, stepping back to let her get dressed.

"I've been in war zones, Ace." Kitty snapped her fingers in what she hoped was a debonair manner. "I can pull off anything."

Kitty hoped she was right, because leaving Ace was going to be the toughest thing she'd done in a long, long time.

* * * *

Ace heard his phone chime, but he was pretty busy pulling rope on a young bull Steele insisted need a practice outing before he bucked in the big show.

Thank God Steele was going to do the test ride, not him. Ace knew the elbow of his riding arm wouldn't take the strain the big Brahman would put on him. Hell, the stupid thing protested when he rode the mechanical bull at his workshops these days.

Steele glanced at him from where he was perched behind the big hump, wrapping his rope around his hand. "If you need to get that, I'll just hang out here, buddy."

"Fuck you, Flannigan." Ace tugged the rope one more time, letting Steele adjust, then slam his fist down on the rope.

"If you two are about to get busy I want to be somewhere else." The stock manager, Troy, stood alongside the chute, stopwatch in hand.

"Hell, if y'all are going at it, I want to be in another state." Coke Pharris spat in the dirt. The barrel-chested bullfighter was ready for action, bouncing back and forth on his toes beside Troy.

"Will you shut up?" Ace climbed down off the rail, clipping the gate rope to the hook, ready to let Steele fly when he nodded. They hadn't really told anyone but the stock contractor about this little test ride, and since Cash was one the Four Horsemen like Ace and Steele — well, he wasn't arguing.

"Just teasing." Steele winked, his grin wild and huge. The man was an adrenaline junkie to this day, retired or not. Steele slid up one more inch on his rope, then turned his head and gave the nod.

For the next eight seconds or so, time seemed to slow down to a crawl. Ace pulled the gate, Purple Rain leaped out of the chute and into an immediate right spin into Steele's riding hand, and Ace clambered up to watch from the fence, a safe distance from the flashing hooves and shiny horns.

The bull had a lot of spin, but not a lot of kick, at least until about six seconds in. Then the big beast seemed to realize that Steele wasn't falling off and the ride changed in tone in an instant. That damned bull put its head down and its back feet went almost vertical, well over the heads of anyone watching.

"Eight!" Troy shouted, and Steele started looking for a place to get off. Coke raced in and tapped the bull on the nose, getting his attention, and Steele blew out the back, his legs coming around in a spinning cartwheel for a moment. The damned fool landed on his feet, though, then ran to the fence and let Ace haul him off the arena floor.

The bull got a little frisky after that, chasing Coke in a tight circle. Coke got in the pocket and spun the monster on a dime while Cash opened the gate to the back of the chutes, where Purple Rain would eventually find himself funneled into a pinch chute so they could remove the ropes and straps and get him loaded back into a pen.

"Good one, Buddy," Ace told Steele, clapping him on the back.

"Thanks." Stele watched Coke and Cash move the bull out of the arena. "Unless he gets better in the first few seconds he's going back down to the little rodeos, though."

"Yeah." Troy joined them, climbing up to sit on the top rail. "So, who keeps texting you?"

"What?" Ace tried for innocent and stupid, opening his eyes wide.

"People call you. They know your hands don't work well enough to text back sometimes." Steele gave him a glinting grin. "Tell."

Ace looked at his hands, which could hurt pretty bad when it was cold and wet. "Yeah, yeah. It's just emails. Now, let it go."

He wasn't sure if he was ready to share Kitty yet. He barely knew her, but she was texting when she was in the States, emailing when she wasn't and occasionally calling. Late at night, when she said the damndest things and made him all hard and sweaty.

Ace kinda adored her.

He wanted to get her to an event, let the guys meet her in person before he told them anything. That would keep them off his back. Steele and Cash, especially, had a tough time talking trash about a lady they'd met.

"You know we'll find out eventually."

"I do. Just not ready to share yet."

"Have you told Lucky?" Steele asked, referring to their other Horseman, the only one of the four who had ever been in a serious relationship.

"Nope." He glared at everyone, even Troy. "Drop it."

To his surprise, they dropped it. Damn, that was some kind of a first, but Ace wasn't gonna look a gift horse in the mouth. When he was ready to share Kitty with the world, he would. Until then, he would watch the news and text her right back, sore hands or not.

Chapter Five

Kitty met the eyes of the man at the door of the Garden, then flashed her press pass. "I have credentials."

"Sorry. No entry," he rumbled.

She raised one eyebrow at the big oaf they had at the fucking door, then she whipped out her phone and texted Ace Porter.

Here. Come get let me in.

Now.

It was cold. She'd been off the plane from Guatemala for about three hours, and she wasn't in the mood to play games with the hired goons.

It figured that Ace would arrange to see her here in the city when she was tired, skinny and her nails looked like hell. At least her apartment was clean so she could have him over after the show without feeling like a slob. She needed to see him. Touch him.

The guy folded his arms and glared at her like all union employees in New York glared at everyone. That lasted all of two minutes, which was when Ace showed up, putting his cowboy boots down hard.

"Let her in, buddy," Ace said, his drawl making it polite but an order all the same.

She let herself glare, but resisted sticking her tongue out. Barely. "Hey. Welcome to New York."

"Yeah. Great weather y'all got up here." The concourse was basically deserted, and as soon as they were away from the security goon, Ace put an arm around her.

"It's perfectly lovely, especially considering I'm coming in from Quetzaltenango." Hot in the day, cold at night—Kitty was grateful she hadn't had to meet Senor Xela during the rainy season.

"Queta-who?" He grinned down at her, his dimples dug deep, the scar on his cheek making his smile crooked.

"Quetzaltenango. Talked to a man who sent a foot to an oil executive's wife as proof of life. Fascinating. Bad teeth. Decent waltzer. How've you been?"

"A foot?" He stopped a moment and stared, something serious flashing in his eyes. "Wow. Been pretty boring here compared to that."

"Well, he didn't send *my* foot." She tried to smile, and almost made it.

"You look like you need some sleep, darlin'." He led her to a medical room with cots and the smell of antiseptic.

"Just jet-lagged. Thanks for the invitation, by the way. I've never watched bull riding before." Kitty honestly didn't know much about it, still. She knew an enormous amount about Ace Porter, however. She knew where he lived—Weatherford—what he drove—a Ford F250—what his mother liked to drink at her favorite bar—caramel appletinis. She knew how much he paid in taxes, how he'd made his money, who he spent money to go and visit and that he dressed left and was very into nipple play.

She was hoping he wanted to go have a nice, long, stress-reducing fuck after he was done working.

She was also hoping that her cameraman Leroy had made his flight back to Houston and wouldn't be crawling down her back all night.

"Not a problem. Figured it was time for you to see what I do. You want to freshen up, this is the place. Before it gets busy in here." Ace bent and kissed her like he meant it.

Oh.

Oh, wow.

With a side of yum and thank God for everlasting lipstain.

His hand slid into her hair behind her head, holding her in place.

Wow.

Again with the wow.

The weekend they'd spent together had left her sore, wrung out, stupid and happy as hell. He hadn't called for days, though, and once he had, they'd had a couple of simple, friendly chats when she was in the country. She'd sent texts and emails and had gotten polite replies. Kitty'd pretty much decided that the chemistry between them had been a figment of her imagination, except for that one conversation they'd had at two a.m. his time, but that had to be an aberration.

She was thinking now maybe not so much. Maybe the man had something for her after all.

His other hand slid down to shove under her ass and he lifted her on one of the gurneys. Oh, yes. She wrapped her legs around his hips, body instinctively trying to get closer. "You taste good, darlin'. Real good," he said.

"And you feel like heaven." She smiled against his lips.

"Oh, now, I'd rather feel like someplace warmer. Where there's sin." He kissed her again, rocking hard between her legs.

His hips spread her wider, that silver belt buckle the only thing harder than the bulge in his jeans.

He was humping against her like there was no tomorrow, like this wasn't the least bit casual. Like he wanted her more than his next breath. God, he was a master at hiding his need over the phone, but hot as the hinges of hell in person.

She was with him, bearing down against him, hips moving faster. "Please."

"Yeah. Yeah. I— Damn." He kissed her throat, her jaw, his hands moving on her now that he didn't have to hold her up.

Her jeans were popped open, his hands nudging in to touch her. She was so wet that he didn't have any problem sliding through her folds, circling her clit.

"So hot." He said it against her mouth, tongue rubbing her lower lip.

She groaned, nodded, her hips moving without her permission, riding Ace's touch as if it was the only thing she could do. One finger slipped inside her, testing her, stretching her. His calluses felt shivery good.

"Want you." She hadn't wanted a man like this in…forever. Hell, this was hotter than their weekend together.

"Now. Yeah?" He reached down for his belt buckle but detoured to his pocket, pulling out a condom. "I was optimistic."

"Yeah. Optimism is a fine quality. Planning, too." She wiggled her jeans and panties off, her heels easily clicking to the floor.

"I think so, too." His buckle opened, his jeans coming down so fast they probably left skid marks. He opened the condom easily, getting himself ready for her.

She moaned and grabbed him, pulled him closer for a kiss. Their lower bodies knew what was what, her pussy sliding along Ace's shaft, making the offer clear. Ace huffed out a happy breath, driving against her, the head of his cock sliding inside her even as his tongue invaded her mouth. Fuck, he was good at that. Kitty bore down, her body welcoming him in. They could have mad-wonderful foreplay later, when they weren't rushing. For now it had been too long. He needed her like no one else, his body deliciously hard. He took her places she'd never even thought of, and she'd let herself believe this wasn't even real.

Her fingers were wrapped around the edge of the gurney frame, her legs wrapped around his waist, heels digging into his ass to pull him closer, deeper.

"Jesus." The word burst out of him and Ace shoved harder, rocking the little gurney thing.

"Harder. Please. I'm right there." She could hear people now, too close, and the naughtiness of it was so hot. Kitty wanted to come, wanted to feel him in her when her inner muscles clamped down.

"Yeah." He ground against her, his pelvis pressing down. He bent to bite at her neck, his mouth moving down.

The tension in her peaked and she bounced a little, whispering his name.

So good. So good.

"God, Kitty. I can't... Gotta..." Ace moved faster, his rhythm breaking down. She loved how his cheek pulled under the force of his emotion, the scar not up to the stretch.

She squeezed him tightly, needing him to come along with her. Ace stiffened, burying his face against her neck, his groan ringing through the room. He was right there, right where she needed him to be.

She hummed through her orgasm, body relaxing, tension melting out of her.

"Y'all have about five minutes before Doc gets here." Someone bellowed it through the door.

Her eyes went wide, laughter bubbling out of her as she clung to Ace's upper arms. "Oops."

"Thanks, Jonesy!" Ace chuckled, bending to kiss her before hoisting himself up and cleaning them like the gentleman he was.

"I hope I won't get you in trouble, Ace." She scrambled down, tugged on her jeans.

"I pay Jonesy's salary." He winked. "And I'm not the first man to bring someone here. Luckily Doc sterilizes." He kissed her again, for what seemed like good measure before straightening his clothes. "I'll show you where you can wash up."

"Thank you." He'd done a good bit with his handkerchief, but a girl liked soap and water.

They looked at each other for a long second, then they both cracked up, laughing so hard the entire arena had to hear it. If this was what bull riding was all about, she'd have to come to the shows more often. She thought she might be able to get used to it.

She cleaned up, freshened her makeup and, thankfully, no one was standing outside staring at them when Ace showed her to seats close to a bunch of monitors and mics.

"I've got to work on camera tonight, but I'll just be over there." There weren't a whole lot of people around yet, only a couple guys warming up in the dirt, running laps.

"Work. I'll pay attention and send Leroy and Honey pictures." She wasn't worried at all. God knew she was self-amusing, and she loved people watching and learning new things.

"'Kay. See you in a bit, darlin'." He kissed her cheek, not a bit self-conscious. She did like a man who was at home in his skin.

Kitty settled in, crossed her legs and grabbed her phone. She needed to call Honey, make sure Leroy was heading home.

She could see men jogging, bouncing up and down, talking to one another. It was kinda hot. Like they were doing calisthenics. Who knew cowboys were so bendy?

"Hello?"

"Hey, Honey! Did Big Daddy make his flight?"

"Hey, girl. I hear that he did. He had a long layover, but he's on his way."

"Good. It was a hard one, this time. He spent a long time alone in a room while guys tried to sleep with me." Unlike being home, where she slept with one within five minutes of saying hello to him.

"Oh, baby, you need a better class of losers." Honey was a hoot, and she sounded just like Aretha Franklin.

"You know it. How're the kiddos?"

Someone out there on the dirt was bouncing.

Up.

Down.

Up.

Down.

People were slowly filing into the building, taking seats. There were lots of skinny, sparkly women with kids in the seats around her. Fascinating. Maybe she should get one of those rhinestone belts.

"Right as rain, baby girl. You should be here. I'm making spaghetti."

Oh, she loved Honey's spaghetti. The woman had been born and raised in Houston, so it tasted kind of like chili with noodles. "Oh, you're a tease. I'm going to grab a beer, then Ace invited me to a late dinner."

She was very curious to see what restaurant was cowboy-appropriate.

"Well, have some amazing dessert for me. You're in New York, after all."

"I will. I love you, lady. Kiss the kids for me. I miss you."

"Miss you, too. Come see me soon."

"I promise." She hung up, surprising herself by tearing up a little. Silly, but she had guilt for keeping Leroy away from his kids for so much time. Still, they treated her like family and she loved them for it.

Ace caught her attention, lights going on where he was standing, holding a microphone. He looked miserably uncomfortable. She gave him the once-over, watched him tip his hat as the crowd roared. Most decorated cowboy in rodeo apparently, and great in bed.

The cowboys were starting to line up along the rail fences, all chaps and hats, protective vests hanging open. Looked like it was almost party time. Fireworks started going off, spotlights swirling around as the announcers announced one man after another. Each cowboy tipped his hat and the crowd roared, and really, it was pretty impressive. The neatest thing was the crowd-watching, though. There were locals dressed in dark denim and artfully done hair, there was the press, there were kids—lots of kids. Then there were people who had to be in the City only for the event— cowboy hats and rhinestones and flat-ironed hair.

All of them squealed at the fire, though. Even the sophisticated New Yorkers.

When the lights came up and the first man came out of the gates and slammed into the dirt, in like two seconds, Kitty started to get intrigued. By bull number four Kitty was fascinated. By round two, Kitty wanted to try it herself. It seemed scarier than hang gliding.

She wondered if Ace would let her do it. She'd bet he'd be amused when she asked.

Every so often she'd glance toward him and he'd be smiling at her, the lines beside his eyes crinkling up. It was nice that he was thinking of her while he was working, though. Of course, he could be checking to make sure no one was coming to take her away for having sex in a public venue. That made her chuckle, made her blush.

Made her a little hot, too.

Time flew by, what with the riding and the clown to watch and the music and all. Before she knew it, it was all over but the autographs.

Ace was right there at her elbow, hand warm and sure. "Hey, darlin'. I am now off the clock."

"Excellent. Did you work hard?" She took his hand, let him stand her up, conscious of all the eyes on them.

"Not so much. Sweaty in the lights, and I need to wash the makeup off." He winked, neatly, steering her up the stairs. Said makeup was nothing but a light sheen compared to what she'd worn on occasion.

"You look exceptional on camera, though." She should know — it was what she did.

"Thanks." They hit the concourse, and Ace headed for the curtained off area labeled 'staff only'. As soon they walked in, someone handed Ace a beer, someone else clapped him on the back.

"Great show tonight, y'all. Good deal," Ace said. He put a hand on her waist. "Come on, there's a dressing room of sorts back here."

"I'm with you."

The clown came up, makeup half off, eyes red-ringed and tired looking. "Ace, call Fred in. Coke's neck is hurt."

"Shit. What happened to Pharris?" The sleek cell phone came out, Ace flipping it open and dialing.

"He got caught by that last chute, Doc's sending him for X-rays."

Kitty winced. *Hospitals. Yuck.*

"Damn it, all." Ace growled into the phone. "Steele. Call Fred up. Get someone at the hospital here, too. We need a go-between for Pharris on the insurance and all. Dillon will be going too." Ace raised an eyebrow at the clown, who nodded.

"Do I need to let you go, Ace?" She would hate to lose out on their evening, dinner and all, but work was work.

"Nope. I just need to handle a few aftershow things, and we'll be good." He grinned, the dimple only on one side this time. "Pharris has the touchiest neck in bull riding."

That made the clown growl, which was part interesting and part terrifying. Clowns scared her a little close up anyway.

"What?" Ace shook his head. "I just mean he's broke it how many... Okay. Well, get his wife over there with him." Ace glanced back at the clown. "Cotton took a helluva knock. You know where Emmy is?"

"Doesn't she work for you?" Dillon asked.

Ace stared at the guy, who stared back. "Jesus, you pay a guy a million and a half a year and he turns into a diva. Go mother hen Coke. Angie! Find Emmy."

Kitty actually chuckled, then her eyes went wide when this amazing, stacked, Bettie Page lookalike sashayed over on six-inch stilettos. "You need me, boss man?"

"No, your hubby does. He's on the way to the hospital. Took a hit back behind the chutes putting a flank strap on, of all things. Steele will run you to the hospital. Take Dillon with you."

"Shit." She reached out, squeezed Dillon's fingers. "Poppy okay?"

"They're gonna do X-rays."

Dillon and who must be Emmy walked off hand in hand and Ace chuckled. "He really doesn't like me."

"The clown? He's good at his job." People didn't like bosses, that was how it worked. She could understand that. "You're a safe target."

"Yeah. Dillon and I get along fine. He's just real protective of the bullfighters. Troy!" The bellow startled her. Startled a big old guy with a barrel chest and a ten gallon hat, too.

"What, you old bastard?"

"I have to go. Personal stuff. You'll hold the fort until Steele gets back?"

The big guy, Troy, looked surprised, but nodded. "You got it."

She noticed that there wasn't any media allowed back here, no press passes. Weird.

Cool.

"Come on, darlin'."

"Hold up, Ace." The big guy came over, boot heels ringing. "Troy, ma'am. Pleased."

"Katherine Carpenter. Kitty. It's nice to meet you."

"Thanks. I liked that piece you did in Los Angeles." He winked. "Too bad Ace here don't watch the news." Someone called Troy's name and the man was off and running again. Well, striding long and tall rather than running.

She blushed, pleased. It was still new enough to be neat when someone recognized her.

Ace raised a brow. "You ready to go, honey?"

"I am. It's busy in here and I'm selfish enough to want you all to myself."

"Yeah." His hand felt warm and right on her waist. "I'm sorry about all the folks."

"Bah. Why?" She grinned at him. "You ever been in a newsroom? They're busy. This is a little like home."

"Nope. I do watch the news, by the way. Dallas." He led her out, waving to a couple of folks, chatting with one more kid with a clipboard who needed him to sign off on something. On the way out of the curtain, though, they ran smack into a broad-chested, Latin-looking cowboy.

"Ace! Amigo. I was looking for you."

Ace sighed. "Hey, Balta. What's up?"

The man flashed her a white-hot, shining smile.

Wow. Pretty.

"Baltazar de Silva. *Bom dia.*" He held out a brown, square hand.

"*Bom dia, senhor. Prazer em conhece-lo.* Katherine Carpenter." Her Portuguese didn't suck entirely.

"Your accent is very nice." Balta smiled, holding her hand an extra second or so, which made Ace pull her close. Cute.

"What do you want, Balta?" Ace asked with the air of a long-suffering man.

Balta launched into a tale of some difficulty with a Brazilian bull rider and his visa, and Ace held up a hand. "I'll call Sandy tomorrow and he can get with the lawyer. Does the kid have somewhere to stay tonight?"

"*Sim. Sim.* He is very young, frightened. He will stay with me and Joa."

"Good. No problem, buddy. I saw him ride. He'll get to stay." Ace clapped Balta on the shoulder. "See you tomorrow."

Ace kept her in the curve of his elbow all the way to the elevator, and it felt amazing — the quiet strength.

"Whew. Man, I need to turn off my cell and hide, huh?" He hugged her tightly once they were in the elevator. "How are you holding up?"

"I'm grand. Thanks for inviting me. It's exciting." *Not whoa, he's going to cut off my fingers exciting, thank God, but whee roller coaster exciting.*

"Cool. I like it." Yeah. Yeah, she could see how he would have been good at it.

They headed down to the street. "Do you need me to get us a cab?"

"That would be great. I don't drive here."

"Neither do I." She headed out, ignoring the random photographers and the rain, whistling loud.

A cab slid to a *slooshing* stop in front of her, and Ace gave her an admiring smile. "Nice."

"I'm a pro. You know where we're going?" She slid in, chuckling as Ace body-checked a guy trying to steal their ride.

"I do." Ace gave the cabbie the address while she marveled that he'd displaced a guy who had at least six inches and fifty pounds on him. That kind of utter male strength and confidence gave her a warm glow.

She scooted closer, smiled. "There were way more women there than I thought there would be."

"Yeah? They're our bread and butter." They were heading toward an area that had a lot of nice little restaurants, nothing fancy, only family-owned kinds of places.

"Really? I guess that's good for the guys. The riders, I mean."

"It is. Mostly. Sometimes it's a big pain in the ass." That was a wry little laugh. "Oh, there. On the left."

Italian. Yum.

He paid for the cab before she could get her wallet out, got her moving under the awning, where he opened the door for her. It was old-fashioned and charming and dear.

"Ace!" A middle-aged Italian man came out and shook Ace's hand, smiling this huge, infectious smile. "Good to see you, my friend. And you bring me a TV star!" The man took her hand and kissed it.

Kitty beamed, holding his hand a moment. "Star is a little bit of an exaggeration, but thank you."

"It is a huge pleasure to meet you. My name is Lucas. I meet Ace here when my son decides to be a bull rider. My son! A New York Italian, huh? Come, sit."

She had to love the way people adored Ace. She got the impression that he knew people everywhere, and could get them to give him the shirts off their backs because he would do the same for them.

"They have Italian bull riders?" That seemed…odd.

"One." Ace winked at Lucas. "He's down in Beaumont this weekend. In the smaller tour."

"He is. He rode. Eighty-three."

After tonight she knew that was a fair score, a decent one.

"Good on him!" Ace touched closed fists with Lucas. "So, you got room for us tonight, buddy?"

"Always. Always. Come. Eat. I have Marco make you special dinners."

"Thanks, man." They went to the table, Ace holding her chair for her.

"Thank you." She lifted her face instinctively for a kiss. He gave it, right there at the table, his mouth brushing across hers. He tasted a little like coffee.

She felt her cheeks warm, heat, her nipples tightening. One little kiss and her body was getting ready for him.

She sat, Ace joining her on the same side of the small table. It felt intimate, as if they had closed the door on the outside world and were hiding together in a garlic-scented magical world.

The wine came, along with crostini and tapenade, and they started nibbling, the flavor of brine and the crunch of the bread making her hum. "What have you been doing, over the last month?"

"Mostly what I was doing tonight. What have you been up to?"

"Working. Traveling. Traveling. Working." She winked. "Exciting stuff."

"Sounds like it. So am I a cretin because I've never seen your show?" Ace did seem a bit chagrined.

She chuckled. "No. I'm on cable, I don't have my own show, and I've been told I look different on camera. I'm going to pretend I'm entirely prettier in person."

"I think you'd be beautiful anywhere." He took her hand, his thumb rubbing over her fingers. "Lord, it's good to see you."

"I was tickled that I'd be in town in time to see you." If she'd switched flights to make sure she could make it, that was her secret, especially since she'd thought he just wasn't that into her. She was a silly romantic at heart.

"Yeah? Well, now you see what I do. Not very glamorous, huh?"

"Ace, I have lived in a tent in the Amazon, I have worn the same flak jacket every day for a month. My job is the big not-glamor."

"Well, you live in New York." He fed her an olive, his fingers slick with the little bit of oil on the plate.

She lapped at his fingertips. "I do. You should come see my apartment."

Fuck me on my bed.

"Yeah? I could do that." His breath hitched and he shifted restlessly, staring at her mouth.

"Excellent. I live uptown." That the apartment was probably smaller than his hotel room was the cold truth of city life.

"Excellent." Ace grinned. "I hope you don't mind that Lucas will give us whatever he wants to eat."

"I don't mind a bit." She was easy when it came to food. "Where do you go next?"

"Connecticut for almost a week. Then home for a rare weekend off." He sounded happy about that, his shoulders relaxing at the very idea, she thought.

"That's sounds happy-making. You have a lot of family close?"

"In Texas? Some, yeah." He tilted his head. "You? You close with your people?"

"No." Her cheeks heated and she forced herself not to look away. "I have Leroy and Honey, though."

Her family had been extremely clear when she'd gone into journalism, and left Missouri, that she could fend for herself. In fact, her extremely conservative father's words were, "If you leave this house without a husband, you will never be welcome back."

He'd meant it, too. Every word. The last Christmas card she'd sent had come back refused.

"Hey, I have some relatives that haven't come out of the trees," Ace said. "No worries."

Their next course came, which was a lovely soup with a tomato base. Polenta croutons and shaved parmesan finished it off.

"This is stunning." She licked her lips, humming over the bright, almost gazpacho flavor. "Do you have brothers and sisters?"

"Three sisters, older. One brother." He winked. "Younger. Kind of a turd."

"Oh, man. I have one brother. Older. Married with children. Unlike me."

He leaned on her a moment, stretching to steal a date wrapped in bacon. "Why not? I mean, not that I'm not glad." His hazel eyes glinted with mischief.

"I was engaged once, for about three months. He found an anchor, and I haven't done a lot of long-term since." Anchors were way better catches than correspondents, she'd found out. Especially when the man in question was a producer. "You?"

"Oh, I'm busy, you know? And I get a little sour on the buckle bunnies who want to get with you and then claim to be pregnant. They just want a catch." He shrugged, sipping the beer Lucas had brought with her wine. "I guess that sounds really women hater of me, and I swear that's not who I am."

"I promise not to turn up with child and tie you down, Ace." She understood busy, and God knew she understood people using someone to get ahead of the game.

"Oh, hey, someday I want kids. I don't see that as the only thing to build on." He winked, nudging her leg with his.

She chuckled, nodded. Someday. "My job description isn't exactly child-friendly, with the bombings and danger and missiles."

"Bombings?" Now she had his complete attention. "Shit, darlin'."

"Twice, yeah. Not my favorite thing." The huge sound of an explosion, shaking of the very ground under her feet... goosebumps rose on her arms. No, not her best memories.

"I bet. I been shot at once."

She was saved from her curiosity by the arrival of the entree, an exquisite fettucine with a flaky white fish in lemon caper sauce. *Uhn.*

"Smells good." She twirled the pasta on her fork, moaning at the rich flavor, the spicy afterburn.

"It does." Ace wasn't eating, though. He was watching her.

"You want a bite?" Kitty asked, holding out her fork.

"Hell yeah." He opened up, ready to bite it off her utensil. *Yum.* Her free hand was on his thigh, sliding as she supported herself. Ace groaned, shifting a little to give her better purchase. "Tastes good."

"It does." God, he smelled amazing, better than the food. "How's yours?"

"I have no idea." He laughed before reaching down and grabbing a noodle with his fingers, then popping it in her mouth. She bit his finger, playfully, jonesing on his laugh. "Ow." He laughed harder, not flinching at all. "Spicy? Lucas usually makes it heavy duty for me."

"It's delicious." Hot, but creamy, too. Filling.

"Cool." He finally forked up a bite of the pasta and nibbled on it, his eyes rolling a little.

She chuckled, dug into her noodles. Bright and tart and eye-crossingly yummy. The somehow delicate but hearty garlic bread was perfect alongside, and the salad came at the end like it did in all excellent Italian meals, cleansing the palate.

The whole thing was perfect—relaxing, filling, and Ace kept her laughing with his stories. He told her all about the Brazilian she'd met, Balta, and how he liked both men and women, and about the big guy Troy and how he liked to play practical jokes.

She responded with stories about her last trip to Argentina, skydiving in New Guinea, how she loved Leroy's house in Houston.

They were laughing right up into the dessert, which was this amazing dark chocolate cannoli, the crunchy shell flaky and brown.

"Oh, god. Look at that..." God, she hoped she had room, because she was eating that.

"We need some coffee, huh?" Oh, Ace was willing to linger. That was a good sign.

"Yes. God, yes. Because that looks amazing." She touched her finger to the chocolate, licked her fingertip clean.

"It is. He uses this really pricey cocoa." Ace watched her mouth intently.

She nodded, gathering any hint of chocolate from her lips. "It's luscious."

Ace picked up a fingerful and held it out to her. "Let me see that again."

Oh.

Flirting.

Hotness.

She leaned forward, licking the end of his finger before she wrapped her lips around it and sucked the chocolate right off. She was talented at this. She knew it, and she wanted to share with Ace, play a little.

Ace moaned a little for her, his mouth open. Good thing they'd both had garlic.

After swirling her tongue around the tip of his finger once more, Kitty backed off, hummed softly. "Yum."

"Wait until you taste the shell." He broke off a piece of crispy pastry, offering that over.

Her teeth sank into her bottom lip, then the little, sweet, needy dance started again.

"I like the little bit of salt he uses." He grinned then licked his lips, looking like the cat with all the cream.

"Mmhmm. You want a bite?" Her nipples ached and she rubbed her thighs together trying to soothe the need building inside her.

"Sure." His head tilted when she offered a little piece, and he nipped at her finger.

She chuckled and slid even closer to him. "Good?"

"God, yes. Now some chocolate." He got an actual forkful and slipped it in his mouth, then kissed her, needy and hard. Kitty melted — Ace was the least self-conscious, most solid man she'd ever met, and he made her burn.

He smiled right into her blinky eyes when he pulled away. "Hold that thought, darlin'. I'm going to get us some of this to go."

"You are a brilliant man." She swayed a little, trying to convince herself that humping a cowboy in a restaurant would be bad for her career.

Lucas gave them a knowing smile along with the coffee and cannoli to go, giving Ace a man hug before letting them leave. "Come back soon, Ace," Lucas said in his booming voice. "I like this lady with you. So good to see you smile."

Ace flushed, but those dimples dug deep into his cheeks and he looked pleased. "Will do! Take me to your place, darlin'?"

"I'd love to." They found a cab and headed uptown, her cheek on his shoulder. He smelled like something that was increasingly home. Like leather and Old Spice and an underlying earthiness that was probably cow.

How did a man who'd been in New York for days smell like the ranch?

Kitty lifted her face, offering him another kiss. Ace took the cue, kissing her good and hard, a nice, thorough exploration. *Beautiful man.*

They pulled up to her building and Kitty slipped the driver his money, the doorman opening the door for them.

"Wow. Swanky." Ace put a hand on the small of her back, letting her lead.

"It's a nice place." She headed up. Her flat was teeny tiny, but it was hers and she made it work as her sanctuary.

She unlocked her door, manhandled it open, then waved him in. The apartment was long and skinny, the walls covered with all the wonders and treasures she'd collected over the last ten years, from African masks to Amazonian statuary.

Grinning, Ace turned in a circle. "Wow. This is like, the size of my kitchen."

"Really?" *Holy moly.* "It's a good size, and there's a view. Come see." She dropped off the cannoli in the kitchenette, then led him around the purple velvet chaise to the one window.

"Oh, this is right nice." His hand slid down to her ass when he stood beside her, staring out at the New York night.

"It's a million-dollar view of the city, or so I'm told." Her eyes closed and her hips rolled.

"Cute." Then he paused before glancing at her and raising a brow. "No shit? Like, for real?"

"Hmm? Yeah, actually. The asking price for this place is three and a half."

"Wow." He genuinely looked shocked. "That's…kind of obscene, darlin'. For that you can buy a big old spread in Texas."

"It's the city. You have to admit it's beautiful."

"It is. Especially from up here." He let her lean against him, absorbing his strength and warmth.

"You smell right." It was important, to like how a man smelled. That it please her, not turn her off.

"You think? I like that about you, too." Ace proved it by nuzzling under her hair, right at her ear, and that little, gentle touch made her gasp. "We gonna have dessert for breakfast and skip right to you showing me that your bed is big enough for both of us?" He bumped hips with her, his dimples springing up.

"That is a wonderful idea." Practically perfect. She really did like the way he put things in such a logical progression.

"Let's go, then." Ace turned her away from the window, his hand sliding up and down her back, tantalizing little touches light as goosedown.

Her bed was hidden by a screen, the posts draped in multicolored silk scarves.

"Pretty. Do you plan to tie me up?" Ace fingered one of the scarves.

"Huh? Oh! No. No, these are only for decoration. They're too itchy to wear, but somehow I get one every time I go to Asia."

"Ah. Well, we can't have itchy." Ace turned her, tilting her face for a kiss.

She wrapped her fingers around his waist, pinkies following the leather belt all the way around as she stepped out of her heels.

Kissing her harder, Ace pulled at her clothes, trying to get to her skin. They'd been idling, but now they'd gone zero to sixty in only a few seconds.

She went up on tiptoe, moaning into those hungry lips. He was so skilled at that kissing thing. Exceptional at the touching, too.

She got his shirt unbuttoned, glided her hands in to touch him, teasing him through his undershirt.

"Feels good, darlin'. Let's get even better." Ace stepped back long enough to pull both his shirts off, then reached for her.

"Oh…" She let her hands slide along those ripped, ridged abs, fingertips circling his nipples.

"Oh, now. No fair." Ace tugged at her clothes. "I want to touch, too."

"I'm a very fair lady." She pulled her blouse off, her black push-up bra showing the girls off to their best advantage. Ace seemed to think so, for sure. He eased his hands under, squeezing a little. Her nipples went tight, vying for attention. He was gratifyingly thorough with his fingers, his lips, and she remembered that, fondly.

Ace bent to kiss the top of one breast, then the other. "Much better."

"I bet I can make it even better." She reached back, unclasped the hook of her bra for him.

"Hell, yes." He immediately moved under her bare breasts, his thumbs rubbing her nipples round and round, calluses catching here and there.

"Oh." The sound was little, breathless, and her eyes went heavy-lidded.

"Uhn." He licked at her skin, down from her collarbone, across the top of one breast then down to her nipple, then he bent her back over his arm to suck at it.

"Ace." She pressed against his head, the short hair tickling her as she held him close, begging him not to stop. His mouth kept moving on her, his fingers sliding down her belly to work at her jeans.

She knew she ought to do the same for him, but she was caught, her fingers stupid and still as pleasure held her.

Her jeans slid down under his touch, his mouth finding her other nipple, giving her the sting of teeth.

She was so hot, wet, that she considered being embarrassed for the half second that she wasn't going out of her mind with pleasure. Then she gave up being modest or worried or whatever — Ace was too damned talented. He rubbed against her, slipping down beneath her undies.

Yes. Yes, please. Kitty cried out, rocked against his touch, her body not able to decide whether she wanted him thrusting inside her or circling her clit. The choice wasn't really hers. Ace moved to her clit, finding it and rubbing until she thought she'd scream.

"Ace." Her hips started moving in time with his touch, her toes curling and grabbing onto the fuzzy rug by her bed.

"Hot for me, darlin'. Wet." Ace grinned, a feral expression that was pure hunger and all male.

"Want…" Heat flooded her and she rode the first wave of orgasm out on tiptoe.

"Oh, you have no idea what I want, Kitty. I missed you. Didn't think I could miss someone I only just met, but I did." He kissed up to that spot under her ear, his one hand between her legs, his other on her breast, teasing her.

She whimpered softly, pleasure taking her. Right now, she'd give him almost anything he asked for, her body on fire for more of what he offered her.

"Here, darlin'." He lifted her and sort of tossed her on the bed before stripping out of his jeans. Lean and tanned and muscled, he was the prettiest man she'd ever seen.

She shimmied out of her panties then reached for him. "Come here?"

"Coming." Ace joined her on the bed, his body sliding against hers all the way up from calves to chest.

"Beautiful." She let her hands trail up and down his spine, fingers massaging as she went.

Ace chuckled, his hips bucking against hers, rubbing his cock between her thighs. Sensual man.

"Hard for me." She appreciated that—his hunger, his need. She reached down to trail a finger over that hardness.

"Have been since you showed up tonight. Even after the first time at the show."

"The first time was only a quick hello." She was ready for a long, hard reconnect. Like their first time together. If every time could be like that she might fall hard for him…

"It was. This time we can take our time." Looked like they were on the same page.

"Perfect." She framed his face in her hands and drew him down into a long, lazy kiss, tongue against his lips. Ace opened right for her, let her taste him. Then he returned the favor, his tongue thrusting into her mouth, the cocoa flavor of him wonderful.

His hands were everywhere—on her nipples, teasing her belly, tapping her clit. His touch was enough to drive her insane. He was damned coordinated for a man who was supposed to be all lost in pleasure. She needed to up her game. Kitty slid out from under him, rolling them until she straddled his hips, her wet curls rubbing against his cock.

There. Better.

Ace blinked at her, his hands settling on her hips. "Well, hey."

"Hey there." She chuckled, leaned down, brushing their lips together.

"I like this angle." One hand lifted her breast, nudging against her nipple, which pressed into his palm, hard as a pebble.

"I. I do, too." Her hips shoved back, dragging her pussy along the entire length of his shaft.

"I bet. You're so sensitive, darlin'. Love how you respond to me." Ace gripped her hips and repeated the move from his side.

"You look amazing in my bed." She bit her bottom lip, shutting herself up.

Stop acting like a lovesick idiot and focus. Naked. Hard, Wanting. With her. That was enough for now.

"Good." He kissed her again and she didn't have to worry about words, because he kept her mouth busy with a slow meld of lips and tongues.

One of her nipples caught between his thumb and forefinger. She felt the tug all the way down to her pussy. He hummed into the kiss, working her flesh like a master. His erection rubbed her unmercifully.

Wasn't she supposed to have the upper hand here? She whimpered as the tip of his cock nudged her clit. Ace grunted, doing it again. He was so hot. Kinda huge, his pulse beating against her most sensitive flesh.

"Want you. Again." She reached for a condom on her bedside table, her fingers shaking.

"Yes. Please," he moaned.

Kitty loved the way his accent made *'please'* into five syllables. She went up on her knees, stroking the condom over his shaft, making sure he felt every inch.

His hips rolled as if he was riding a horse, proving that she'd done a great job. "Kitty…"

"Yes." She rubbed the tip against her folds, teasing both of them.

"Fuck. Oh, fuck, darlin'. Let me in." Ace tugged at her hips, trying to work her lower on his shaft.

Kitty nodded, sank down on him, the tiny ache from their lovemaking earlier making it all the hotter. Groaning, he thrust into her, his hands like vises on her skin.

As hard and fast as it had been before the event, this time was just as needy, their bodies both knowing exactly what they needed. *So much for all the time in the world.* Ace grunted, speeding up, his body rocking under her.

Her hands were on his shoulders, her entire body bouncing on his. His gaze traveled from her face to her breasts and Ace made this amazing noise and bucked against her, his hands trying to move, but seeming unable to let go of her hips. She leaned down, knowing what he wanted, what she wanted, stretching so his lips could find her nipple. He closed his lip around the tip, his tongue flicking back and forth. It made her shiver, made her clamp down around his cock, which she would swear swelled harder inside her.

"Oh, God. Ace." She moved harder, her body on fire for him. "Right there."

He nodded a tiny bit, which made his teeth scrape over her skin. Kitty exploded, fingernails digging in as she came around his cock. Ace's head snapped up and he stared right into her eyes when he came, his whole body quaking like an aspen in a storm.

"Wow." She eased herself down against him, heart slamming in her chest.

"Double wow. Bed's not bad." Ace grinned, those dimples irresistible, his hazel eyes so dear and familiar so darned soon.

"Thank you. I like it." She kissed the place the scar ended at the corner of his mouth.

"Mine's bigger. You should come see the ranch."

"I'd love to. You're in Texas, near Dallas?" Leroy lived in Houston, so she knew the heat and humidity of Texas, but not much else. Traffic. Enormous traffic even at two in the morning.

"I am. Weatherford." He stroked her back, helping her settle more comfortably.

"Can you stay the night? I make a mean cup of coffee."

"I can. I'll have to make a few calls." Ace grimaced, but it was comical, not really unhappy.

She chuckled. "No stress. Whatever's easiest."

"I'd like to stay. I don't have to be at the arena until eleven-thirty. We still have dessert for breakfast."

"Dessert." She couldn't hide her grin, imagining the fun time she'd have licking cannoli cream off his skin.

"Second dessert, even." He eased her hair back behind her ear. "I like a lady who isn't afraid to eat."

Kitty nodded. "You never know when you'll have to eat something awful. Enjoy the good stuff." She was incredibly lucky she had a super-revved metabolism.

"You know it. Some days you get the steak, some days you get the mountain oysters."

"Exactly. Today? Totally steak."

"Hell, yes." Ace kissed her, and she knew they were in total agreement.

Chapter Six

Ace woke to the familiar tinny, scratchy sound of *Waltz Across Texas* playing somewhere near his ear. His cell going off. He leaned up on one elbow, trying not to smoosh Kitty, who was right there, snuggled up. *Fine woman.*

"'Lo?"

"So, I hear that a certain skanky ho cowboy was caught having wild monkey sex in sports medicine with a mystery girl and is not in his hotel room having coffee with his buddy."

Steele. Fucker.

"Yeah. You have stinky feet. She doesn't." Coffee sounded just about right, though. Ace could definitely go with some caffeine.

"No shit? We all thought you were queer. She a Yankee?" Steele's voice rang with suppressed laughter.

"Fuck you, and no. She's from St. Louis. She lives up here now."

"Huh. Sports medicine? Really?" Steele's laughter bounced into his ear, the jibes happy, though, not mean.

"What? It had been weeks." He wasn't gonna be ashamed. Steele Flanagan had done the nasty in the bed next to Ace when he was passed out drunk. It took a lot of skank to top that.

"Poor baby. I'll take your spot at the fan meet this afternoon."

"Yeah?" Hell, that was decent. That meant he didn't have to be in until about three. "I owe you one. She's the lady with the texts and emails."

"Shit, you owe me beer and details."

"Yeah, yeah. Go away." He hung up, tossing the phone back on the night table and pondering food.

Kitty cracked one eye open, smiled at him. "People checking to make sure you didn't get lost in the big city?"

"Something like that, yeah." She sure was pretty with morning hair. Ace could get used to seeing her like this.

She kissed his nose. "Coffee and pancakes?"

"You read my mind, darlin'." He loved pancakes. Blueberry. Pecan. Plain.

Kitty stood, grabbed a tiny silky robe and headed the three steps to the kitchen...area.

The place was just tiny. He could cook from the bed. There was a bitty velvet loveseat, a TV, a bunch of yarn, a treadmill and the bed. His guest room was bigger.

"What's the yarn for?" His momma made afghans. Terrible ones. He wondered what Kitty made.

"Hmm? I knit for stress relief. Sweaters. Hats. Socks. It's a thing." She had a tiny, half-sized fridge, and she pulled out eggs and milk.

"Knitting. That's with the two sticks, right?" He watched her ass sway back and forth, happy as a clam.

"It is." The smells of coffee started, then she bent over to dig out pancake mix and he got to watch that tiny robe slide up and up.

Bing. Heaven. Right there. Ace cleared his throat. "Can I do anything?"

"Nope. Just keep me company." She poured and cooked, little butt swinging as she stirred.

He liked to watch her stir. A lot. He wasn't a perv, not really. He was a perv for her. She made his brain go to its caveman place, like his lowest common denominator.

"Do you cook a lot?" She glanced over her shoulder, smiled at him. "Black coffee, right?"

"Right." He pondered that. "I mostly grill. I can make basic shit for sides."

His phone rang again, the waltz seeming to mock him a little. Ace looked at the glowing screen. His buddy Cash. He didn't answer.

Then Kitty's phone started ringing and she grabbed it. "Hey, Big Daddy! You make it home to your wife?"

Cash called again while Kitty was chatting.

Fucker.

Sighing, Ace went ahead and answered. "Hello?"

"Who is she? She's not with the tour," Cash said.

The smell of coffee filled the air as Kitty handed him his cup.

"No, she's not." They shared a grin, him and Kitty, and she turned away to answer some question on her call. "You're nosy."

"No shit. I'm also bored. Who is she? Steele didn't get a name, but Troy says she's the tiny little reporter from that cable news deal, the one that don't suck."

"Troy's right. And you keep your mouth shut." Ace rolled his head on his neck. "You're cutting into my pancake time, buddy."

"Restaurant or homemade?"

Nosy asshole.

"Homemade. There's stirring."

"Oh. See you in Topeka, friend. Have a good one." The line went dead. Cash was a smart man.

Kitty was laughing, tying up her hair. "…not going to Mexico for another few weeks, now. You work on your honey-do list."

Ace tossed the phone at the table again, then thought better of it and grabbed it, turning the ringer off.

Kitty hung up on her call as well, then brought him a plate of pancakes on a tray with syrup and butter on the side. "Ta-da!"

She looked pleased as punch.

"Yum." Ace patted the bed next to him, wanting her closeness as much as he wanted breakfast. "Come share."

She grabbed her coffee and slipped in next to him, her breasts soft and warm against his arm. "I hope you like them."

"What's not to like? Pancakes with butter and syrup? You bein' right here next to me?" He cut the first bite, offering it to her. His momma had raised him right, damn it. Breakfast in bed was hers to start off.

She blushed so pretty, and he liked that there was the barest hint of pale freckles across her nose. She opened up, humming over the bite. Beautiful woman. He loved the way her eyes crossed.

"You next." She stole his fork, leaned in and offered him some, her robe parting in a slow slide that caught his attention, his mouth falling open a little.

He stared, but took the bite when she popped it between his lips. Oh. Those were luscious.

The next mouthful involved a drip of syrup that landed on his belly and her hot little tongue lapping it up.

Fuck. His muscles drew up tight, his cock rising easily in a rush that left him breathless. She got to him in this insane way.

"Sweet." She dragged her finger through the syrup, offered it to him to lick clean. She was so tactile.

He sucked that syrup right off. "Yeah. Good."

Took them a while, but they finished the food, she got them both another cup of coffee, settled close beside him again.

"So, what are you going to Mexico for?" Ace asked, trying to learn more about her instead of jumping her like a sex fiend.

"Work." She sighed. "I'm working on an interview with the head of one of the larger cartels. He likes blondes."

"Cartel?" Ace frowned. "That sounds dangerous, darlin'. I'm not sure that's wise."

She nodded, shrugged. "That's what they pay me to do, though."

He wasn't sure he liked the idea of that. He figured it really wasn't his place to say, but he sure wanted to. "So was that your... I know you told me, but I forgot. Big Daddy." He was her what? Her man Friday?

"Cameraman. Leroy. He lives in Houston with his wife and kids."

"Oh, right. See, I knew you told me." Ace sipped his coffee, luxuriating in being with her.

"He's a good guy, a little bit of a mother hen, but fun and solid. They're my family."

"That's cool. My calls? Two of my three best friends. Nosy buttheads. The ones in the poster, actually."

"Oh." She pinked, her cheeks flushing as if she had a sunburn. "People teasing you about yesterday?"

"A little, yeah. Mostly nosy. We've known each other for years and they want to know everything."

"That's neat. I don't have many old friends that I'm still in touch with." She shoved her hair over her shoulder.

"No?" He'd bet in her line of work people came and went fast.

"I work in a cut-throat field. I have buddies, though. Manicures, massages, wine and chocolate. Girls' night."

"Well, everyone needs that." He guessed. He liked a massage now and then, and he and Cash and Steele could tear it up with a few beers. Ace took her coffee cup and set it aside with his, feeling like maybe they'd talked enough.

He thought she was listening, too, because she opened the tie of her robe, slid under the covers with him.

"I do like your bed, honey." Ace snuggled up, right and tight.

"It's comfy." Her leg dragged along the outside of his, her skin so smooth compared to his.

"It is. It has you in it." He let his hands wander, one on her back, one on her front, exploring the way her body dipped and curved.

That made her smile and they started kissing again, long, slow, maple-flavored kisses that got him riled.

He could kiss her all day. Hell, he could do most anything with her all day. That was a little scary. Her nipples fascinated him, tiny and hard and tight and so fucking sensitive. Ace bent to lick at one, driving her breast up to meet his mouth. Sweet. Sticky, too, a little.

"Ace." She made the prettiest sounds, his name on her lips exciting, necessary.

"Look at you." He wanted her to know how beautiful she was to him.

She arched into his mouth, her nipple nudging his lips. "Flatterer."

"No, darlin'. It's the truth." He bit down, just a little, knowing the sting would send her flying.

Her fingers found his head, her hips rolling toward him. "Yeah."

"So sensitive." He said it against her skin even as his mouth headed across to her other breast, ready to offer the same pleasure.

"Yes." She made the best sound when he found her nipple. Ace eased her down on her back, his legs slipping in-between hers, his mouth moving strongly. Sucking.

Her hot, wet curls moved against his thigh, his hip, his cock. She was on fire for him, and Ace couldn't really remember ever having a woman so honest, so true to her own need. Her body burned against his and she grasped his shoulders, his head.

He nudged that hard nipple back and forth with his tongue then blew on it, blowing air over it.

She arched, heels digging into the mattress, body pressing into him. *Sweet.* Ace moved down a little with his hips, rocking back and forth.

He could tell she was close—could smell her need, her want.

Ace drove harder against her, knowing he'd never make it inside before she went off like a rocket.

He let one hand shove between her legs, fingertips playing her clit, slipping over her wet folds. He circled her nub until she cried out, her body shaking for him, her breath huffing out.

Pretty lady. He loved to watch her come.

Ace waited out her orgasm before rising up and sliding his cock along her, wanting in. His turn, and she spread for him, easy as pie.

God, she felt good. Soft and womanly and a perfect fit for him.

He sank into her, her cunt slick and wet, surrounding his cock.

"God." He was about to start babbling, which was so not him, so he kissed her instead to shut himself up. No saying things he wasn't ready to say.

Her tongue moved against his, her nipples rubbed against his chest and her legs wrapped around his hips.

She held on like he was the hottest thing ever, and Ace was pretty convinced she was the hottest thing since sliced bread. He could get used to this. She was revving up for her third go-round, too, hips bucking, riding his cock.

Ace moved faster, his balls drawing up tight, his belly feeling hard like a board. He needed to come. Soon.

Kitty forced one of her hands between them, touching him, touching herself.

"Oh, Christ." Ace bucked, electric shocks running right through him.

"Close. Again." She bit her bottom lip, moving under him like a fractious pony.

"Yes. I. Oh." He was losing his ability to talk. Damn. Now he didn't have to worry a bit about babbling.

Their lips crashed together and she moaned for him, her sweet cunt rippling around his erection, drawing his need to the surface.

Ace tried real hard not to bite down on her lower lip when he came, even though he gripped her butt hard enough to bruise. He fell over the edge, his cock aching a little with the force of his balls emptying.

She panted for him, lips open against his as they shivered.

"God, darlin'. You make me a little crazy."

"Just a little?" She actually chuckled for him, even if the sound was utterly breathless.

"Maybe a lot. I like it." He'd always been fond of a little craziness, and he was already more than fond of Kitty. She scared the ever-loving shit out of him.

She cuddled in, cheek on his shoulder.

His hands found her back, stroking up and down. Her skin was warm, a little damp. Damn, she was something.

Ace deliberately stayed away from looking at the clock. He didn't want to know how little time he had left with her.

Just like he didn't want to think about how she'd gotten to him so bad that he hadn't even used a rubber. They would have to talk on it at some point, but for now, he could pretend they had a month of Sundays to love on each other.

Chapter Seven

"You got your passport? Your recorder?" Leroy asked.

"Yep. I have mints, granola bars and an extra handcuff key I can hide in a body cavity, too." Kitty did love to tease the big guy. Leroy was like a really protective older brother. He was allowed to give her shit, but no one else was allowed to mess with her. They'd met at the check-in counter in Houston, ready to head to Mexico, and she could tell Leroy was worried about this trip.

Kitty was, too, truth be told. She had always been pretty cavalier about her own safety, but these days she had someone she wanted to see when she got back to the States. She wanted to get in and out of Mexico in one piece, and the cartels were serious business. That was why the network was sending her, she thought. Her contact said the subject of her exposé liked fluffy girl reporters, and she could bat her eyes and wiggle with the best of them.

"I don't like this one, Kitty. I really don't."

"You didn't like Baghdad either, and look what that did for our careers."

"Right." Leroy had the most expressive eye roll she'd ever seen. "You remember that hotel that got bombed, right? When we were on the eighth floor."

Kitty waved a hand. "It took out the lobby. We were upstairs."

"You got a funny way of looking at things," Leroy complained.

"You love it. The adrenaline. The rush. Admit it."

Leroy paused in the action of pulling out his passport, meeting her gaze with his. "I tell you what, and this is the God's honest truth. I used to love it, for sure. I'm getting older, though, and can't run like I used to. I worry what will happen to Honey and the kids if something gets me."

"I can see that. We'll be careful." The thought of doing this job without Leroy kinda panicked her. She leaned on him a lot, and counted on him to be the voice of reason and safety.

"I know we will." He gave her a wide, white grin. "Honey packed my Kevlar undies."

"She knows how to protect the important parts, I can tell." They handed over passports and travel documents, both of them skipping checking a bag. This was a low equipment assignment.

"She has her priorities," Leroy agreed.

They headed for the security line after they got their boarding passes, and Kitty's phone chimed, the text notification the jingle of spurs. Ace. She tugged her phone out to check it.

In Mexico yet?

She grinned, and her fingers flew when she replied.

About to get on a plane.

Be safe.

I'll do my best. Dessert together soon?

You know it.

The immediate assent made her smile, and when nothing else slid across her screen, she tucked away her phone.

Leroy stared at her patiently, waiting, and Kitty tried to ignore him.

"You gonna tell me?" he asked.

"I'm trying not to jinx it, Leroy. I like him a lot."

"Well, you know I'm here if you need me. I'm your buddy."

"I know." It was time to take off the shoes and pull out her laptop. "I promise to fill you in once I know what we're going to be, if anything."

"Is he stringing you along?"

"No. If anything, I am him." She put her belt in the bin, the rhinestones glued on it making her laugh. Sparkly, and a gift from Ace. "I got this, Big Daddy."

"Okay. This is me dropping it, but it will come back around, you know."

"It always does." Leroy was tenacious as a bulldog, which was one of the reasons Kitty adored him, but he would drop the bone for a bit.

They really needed to get through security, after all. Thank goodness that made it harder to talk.

* * * *

"Did you know that Ace doesn't really text?" Steele told Emmy, grinning like a monkey while Ace laboriously typed out a message on his phone.

"I did know that," Emmy said, nodding sagely. Ace could see the twinkle in her eye when he glanced at her out of the corners of his. "When I text he sends back 'Call'."

"Really?" Steele made a sound of amazement. "He sends me 'FU'."

"See how he is?" Emmy laughed. "Boss, we need a few minutes of your time, please."

Ace flipped them both off to finish his text to Kitty about this little Greek restaurant he'd found in Kansas City. He would bet she liked baklava.

Then he shoved his phone into his jeans pocket. "Okay, what?"

"Is it true that she's a TV reporter?" Emmy asked. "I think I've seen her."

"Why is everyone so curious about my — sex life?" He almost said love life, but it might be too early for that. Sex they had, in spades. The rest was allowed to take time, even if Ace was an impatient man.

"He said sex!" Steele crowed. "I told you he was doing it. Our little boy is finally doing it."

Ace glared at Steele, then focused his ire on Emmy. "Who am I, Emmy?"

"The Boss. King of the Cowboys, Ace Porter." She saluted like the 40s sailor pin-up girl she resembled today. "I do not mock. I need to know what my budget is for the new Futurity website."

"Aw, man, did I miss a budget meeting?" Steele asked. He was on the damned board, but he never bothered to show up.

"You did. You have three thousand to play with, Em, and I want to talk to you about revamping the rider search. Pencil me in for Monday."

"You want me to stay here an extra day or are we conference calling?"

"Let's stay here. Clear it with Margeann." Margeann was the lady at headquarters who made all the travel arrangements."

"I'm on it." She winked. "And go you. I hope she's the one, Boss."

"Thanks." He waved her off, then wheeled around and poked Steele in the chest. "My lady is not for general discussion, Steele."

Steele's eyes went wide. "Hey, I was just teasing."

"Well, don't."

"She must be something." Nodding slowly, Steele held up his hands as if to surrender. "I'll be good."

Ace relaxed enough to grin at Steele. "Thanks. I need to make a couple of calls. See you in a bit."

Steele clapped him on the back and Ace walked away, his shoulders still a little stiff. God, he was wound up tighter than one of them monkey toys that beat the cymbals.

His phone rang and he grabbed it eagerly, frowning when it wasn't Kitty. The number looked to be Lucky, who called from a bar on the beach in Mexico when he needed some people time.

"Hey," Ace answered. "You okay, buddy?"

"I am. Tell me about this girl."

"Oh, Christ." Figured that Cash and Steele had let Lucky know something was up. "I forgot to use a condom," Ace blurted.

"Must be serious, then."

"Well, I hope so, but she's sure playing it close to the chest."

"Huh. They're usually all over you." Lucky chuckled. "Serves you right. Hey, can you wire me a little out of my account? I need to fix the outdoor shower."

"Sure, buddy." Ace handled all of Lucky's investments. "You should come out to the ranch sometime soon."

"I probably should. I like being off the grid. Good luck with the lady, though."

"Thanks. She's in your neck of the woods, not mine." He hated that Kitty was in Mexico risking her life, but she sure loved her job.

"Mexico, huh? What is it she does?"

"She's a reporter." Hard-core, serious shit. The idea made him so damned proud, but scared him to death.

"Nice." Lucky sighed, and Ace once again missed his laughing, carefree friend. "Be careful with that condom thing. If she's a career lady she won't want the complications."

"Neither do I, I promise. I miss your face, Lucky. Don't be a stranger."

"You know what, you ought to come down here for a long weekend. Tequila. Sponge cake. Outdoor showers."

"You just want me to come fix shit for you." The idea had promise, though. Kitty was in Mexico, so maybe he could check in on her. Discreetly.

"I might do that. I'd love to see you."

"Yeah, yeah. Just call the cantina. Great chatting. Bye."

Lucky always hung up when someone got maudlin. Ace chuckled and put his phone away. He'd get with Margeann and get a ticket to Mexico. What the hell. Not right now, though. Right now it was time to stop worrying about Lucky and Kitty and get back to work.

Chapter Eight

"*Gracias, Señor.*" Kitty managed a smile, nodding to the cartel enforcer, Carlos, as she grabbed her bag out of his hands. All she had to do was hold it together long enough to get into the cantina.

That was it.

Eight steps. Maybe ten.

Leroy was in there, waiting for her.

Her subject, Marcos Guittierez, gave her a slow, slimy smile and Kitty reminded herself to meet his eyes, smile warmly, turn and walk away nonchalantly.

No running.

She got to the door of the cantina, let it swing shut behind her, and suddenly Leroy was there, huge and dark and worried, wrapping her in a hug.

"Big Daddy." Kitty burst into exhausted tears, a habit she'd never been able to break, damn it.

"I got you, girl. I got you." One huge hand patted her back. "Been waiting for you."

"Good. That was…intense."

"He didn't touch you, did he?" Leroy's face darkened in a deep frown. He'd hated leaving her alone with the jerk. "I could still kill him."

"There was a lot of chase the blonde around the desk, but no touching. No. Just a lot of posturing and sleeping with my back pressed to the door."

A lot of worrying and taking showers with her panties still on and way too many weapons on display for comfort.

"Did you get a decent story?" He sat her down on a stool, ordering, "*Dos tequilas*."

She nodded. "I got a lot. Enough that I was scared, huh? Don't think we need to stay in town tonight." These men had guns, armies, power, and Marco wanted her.

"Okay, honey. Okay." Leroy peered behind them. "You ought to know, though, you got an admirer here, too."

"What? Tell me there aren't more goons." She was holding it together.

Barely.

"Nope. Some cowboy. He's been hanging around for days. Showed up about two days after they kicked me out."

"Cowboy?" She frowned, lifted her head and looked around. Her eyes popped when she saw not just any cowboy, but her cowboy. Oh, for heaven's sake. What on earth was Ace Porter doing in Mexico?

Her eyes went wide, then she stared at Leroy. "I. He asked about me?" How had Ace known where to find her?

"Yeah. He figured it out when, uh, I was drunk and talking shit how I was going to go get my girl out of cartel hell..." Leroy's eyes rolled a little.

"Oh, Daddy. You're so bad." She met Leroy's gaze. "Do I look okay? I'll go say hi." And bye. She needed some downtime, and while she adored Ace, she might lose it if she had to be nice to anyone right now.

"You look fab. You brought waterproof mascara." He patted her back.

"Of course. I was raised right." She squeezed his knee. "Don't leave?"

"Not a chance."

Ace was watching her when she turned around, eye lines crinkled up. And not with a smile. More a squinty frown.

She headed straight over to him, keeping her face cool, calm. Collected. She was still in work mode, after all. "Hey, cowboy. I didn't expect to see you here."

"I know." Ace did offer a smile then, nodding toward Leroy. "I was surprised to find out that was your Leroy."

"My source didn't want him there for the interview."

"Your source. Jesus, darlin'." Ace put his hand on her cheek, thumb rubbing as if she had a streak of dirt on her face.

She closed her eyes for half a second, leaned into his touch for a heartbeat then she stood up. Strong. Confident. "What are you doing here?"

"Visiting a buddy. Trying to get him to come back to the world a little." Ace paused, seeming uncertain for the first time since she'd met him. "Listen, I couldn't help but hear you needed a place to stay."

"Oh, don't worry about me. We'll find something." She was nothing if not resourceful, and she was also determined not to get too used to having Ace around.

"I know. Look, no strings attached. My buddy is way off the grid, and he can put you both up for a couple of days."

"I couldn't put anyone out." Her hands were starting to shake. She needed to get away from all the prying eyes and have a cry.

"You won't." His hand fell to her shoulder. "Come on, darlin'. No one bothers Lucky."

"I… Let's talk to Leroy." She needed to sleep and have something not tequila to eat.

"Sure." He took her arm, his fingers warm and gentle and not slimy. Why did he have to be so nice when she was trying to be no-strings woman?

She took him across the bar. "Leroy? You know Ace Porter?"

"Yeah." Leroy shook hands with Ace. "We met."

"He says his friend has a place we can stay for tonight." That would be better than any fleabag, flimsy hotel they might find, right? Right. She could do this.

Leroy studied her for a moment before nodding. "Okay. Sounds good."

"Can we go now?"

"Sure." Ace and Leroy flanked her, which made her feel safer than she had in days. Leroy carried her bag, Ace was right there, and Kitty could breathe. Really breathe for the first time in five days.

There was a Jeep sitting a block from the cantina and Ace took them right to it, handing her into the front seat.

"My stuff's in the rental truck. I'll follow you. You okay, baby girl?" Leroy asked.

Leroy seemed so serious, so sincere, and Kitty surprised herself by nodding. "I'm safe with Ace."

"I'll drive slow. There's a creek that's dicey," Ace told Leroy.

"Just let's go." Kitty reached out, twined their fingers together.

Ace nodded, starting the engine and waiting for Leroy to get settled in the rental SUV before pulling out.

Kitty took a deep breath, closed her eyes, and held on.

* * * *

Ace pulled up at Lucky's, his hand aching a little. It was hard to drive over rough terrain and hold hands light enough not to wake the lady. Thank God he'd taken his rental Jeep, which was an automatic, rather than Lucky's more reliable Land Rover.

Leroy pulled right up behind him, lights going off. "This place is remote, man. I can see why no one would bother the guy."

"And the owner has a shotgun." Lucky stepped out of the little ramshackle beach cottage with said gun in hand. "Everything okay, buddy?" he asked Ace.

Ace grunted an assent. "Can you find a place for Leroy here to bunk down? Miss Out Cold can come with me."

"Sure, if you don't mind rustic." Lucky looked at Kitty, one white blond eyebrow lifting. "She okay?"

"Wore out, is all. I bet she hasn't slept in days."

Leroy frowned, staring back and forth between Ace and Kitty. "She can bunk with me."

Laughing, Lucky shook his head. "Ace has the not-as-falling apart guest house. You can have my bed and I'll take the couch. I'll fit—you won't."

Leroy's frown got deeper, but when Ace leaned into the Jeep and lifted her she flowed into his arms, not even waking up.

Couldn't argue with that.

"If you need me, holler," Lucky murmured, nudging Leroy inside. Ace could hear Leroy complaining, but what he felt was Kitty, warm and light in his arms, trusting him.

He carried her to the 'guest house', which was actually a nicely done up platform tent. It even had enough room for a chemical toilet and a tiny washstand. The shower was that outdoor contraption Lucky had been talking about.

Her eyes fluttered open as he laid her down. "Ace."

"Hey, darlin'. Do you need a T-shirt to sleep in?"

"Hey. Yeah." She smiled at him, her eyes so bruised with dark circles that he wanted to hit something. "I fell asleep on you. I'm sorry."

"That's okay." He kissed her cheek and tucked a strand of hair behind her ear. "You feeling any better?"

"Yeah. Much. I was okay, just" — she waved one hand, her smile wry now — "tired."

His fucking heart had stopped when he'd seen her launch herself at Leroy, crying so hard. She'd seemed well and truly scared.

That was why he hadn't... Well, they'd called and texted some, but they hadn't been together. Not since New York. She'd called, and Troy had showed Ace some of her news stories.

Ace hadn't figured it would be fair to let himself get too crazy about her and want her to do less than her best at her job to make him happy. She put herself in harm's way for a living. Sooner or later he'd get growly and demand she quit, and it would all go south. Course, that was hard to remember when she was smiling at him like that, looking pale and kinda fragile and all too his.

"This is a neat little beach house." *Okay. Shit.* That was unexpected. She was a city gal these days, right? Used to room service and manicures. Oh, he knew she wasn't pretentious, but Lucky's place was way out there.

"It's not bad. Lucky's been working on improving it enough for the four of us old buddies to have a place to hide out." He handed her the shirt. "I was sure surprised to see your Leroy here."

"Yeah. He was supposed to come on site with me, but it didn't happen that way. He hates being stuck on the outside. Makes him crazy." She stripped off the button-down she wore, slipped off a little lace bra, and tugged his T-shirt on.

Ace tried hard not to stare. "You want anything to drink, darlin'? I got a cooler, or a camp stove. I can make hot water real quick..."

"I'm okay." She dug around in her duffel, pulled out a pair of shorts, and undid her slacks.

"I have cheese and crackers, too." He needed to do something, so he got her some kind of Mexican juice and some cheese and crackers.

She took the snack and the juice, smiled at him again. "Thank you."

"No problem. The bed is a double. Is that okay? I could get a sleeping bag from Lucky." He just...he wasn't gonna be slimy. He'd been the one to avoid that kind of closeness lately, even when they'd been close enough around the country to see each other.

Her cheeks went pink. "Ace, I swear, I won't. I mean, I'm not going to molest you, huh? If you're uncomfortable with me here, I'll stay in Leroy's car for the night, but I can keep my hands to myself."

"No! No, way. I only. You said that drug feller was slimy, and I didn't want you to be worried. You can molest me whenever you want." His ears heated. Lord. Had he said that? Where had his brain gone?

Kitty blinked at him, one eyebrow arched. "Ace, you're not slimy, and I get that... I mean, you don't have to worry about not wanting to get together again or anything. It happens. Chemistry and stuff."

"Oh." *Oh, shit.* "It ain't that I don't want to, which is hard to believe I know. That ain't the problem. I like you a hell of a lot, Kitty. So much that I ain't sure I can deal with your job." There. He prided himself of being honest.

She got a sad expression for about a second, then it disappeared, her expression brightening. "So, don't deal with it. I mean, I'm not at work right now."

"No. No, you're not." Bless her. He grinned and sat next to her on the bed. "I like the shirt better on you."

She grinned back at him, drank about half the juice. "You think?"

"I do. You fill it out nice." He grabbed a piece of cheese.

"Yeah?" She looked down, chuckled. "One day I'll go get them…plumped up, but I'm not ready yet."

"Plumped up?" Ace stopped with the cheese halfway to his mouth, horrified by the very thought. "Why?"

"Because they're little and a bit bigger looks better on camera." She shrugged, the move slow, philosophic. "Right now I'm in flak jackets and fatigues, but when they decide they want me in dresses and suits, they'll want them fixed. Not porn star big, but permanent Victoria Secret big."

"Get a push-up bra." That wasn't right, asking her to get them done. Not when those perky tits were so damned perfect just as they were.

Kitty let out a warm chuckle. "I have a collection of push-up bras. Many colors. You'd approve."

"I so would." He'd seen the black one. "Come here." He couldn't sit there with her and not hold her. It felt right—that she didn't hesitate, simply jumped into his arms with a soft little sound.

Ace held on, stroking her back with one hand, then her hair. "I got you, darlin'."

"You still smell good," she murmured, her breath hitching.

"So do you." Her job wasn't so bad, right? That was his theory when she was this close, at least. God, he wanted her right where she was forever. His brain battled with his heart, both of them telling Ace he was a fool.

"Kiss me hello?"

"Hey, there." Ace kissed her hello and hi and maybe woo hoo, too.

They fit together, hand in glove, her belly soft and warm against his, her butt snuggled against his thighs.

She tasted like heaven, and Ace gave up logic for a bit.

Kitty kissed him like she'd been thinking on it for days, weeks, her tongue sliding into his lips.

He'd been thinking on it since the last time. Shit, that was why he was in Mexico. Running away from her and trying to find her. He rocked with her, his hips starting to thrust.

"Want you."

God, she was pure sex, her nipples rubbing up on his chest even through the shirt.

"You sure? You're not too tired?" He wouldn't be able to stop if they started.

She chuckled. "I can sleep later. You're here now."

"I am. Oh, god, I am." He took his T-shirt off her, needing her skin against his, smooth and creamy and sweet as peaches.

Her laugh was amazing, almost as wonderful as that lean little body, those tight, dark nipples that felt so right to his tongue.

He kissed her mouth, his thumbs finding her nipples. She was so narrow that he could almost wrap his other fingers around her ribs.

His girl. He knew the thought was ridiculous—knew it—but it was true. Every time he tried to deny it he came right back to the certainty of it.

She knew it too, instinctively, he thought. No one could move on him that way and not know it. Kitty moaned for him, fingers working the buttons of his shirt open while she writhed.

Ace helped, moving to let her ease the sleeves down his arms. Oh, hell yes. Now they both had bare skin.

"Ace. So warm." Her belly slipped against his and he could feel her heat through the soft shorts.

"Love how you feel. Love your skin." He shoved at her shorts, wanting the rest.

She wriggled out of the bottoms, naked curves on his lap. He could eat her up. Ace slid one hand down between them, between her legs, touching her where she was so hot, so wet. Oh, she was ready for him.

The sounds she made had his cock raring to go, and when he circled her clit, she bucked in his arms.

"Kitty. Help me." Ace needed out of his pants. He had to get where he could rub against her.

"On it." She fumbled with his buckle, his belt. "Fucking starched denim."

"I know. I can't help it." He was a cowboy, right? Lord. They finally got his jeans open and down and he pulled her back into his lap.

Her fingers were on his cock, palm rubbing over the tip.

"Oh, god." His body shook, his breath catching in his chest, her touch driving him out of his mind.

"Mmhmm." She did it again, and again. Fuck, that was maddening.

"I don't. Kitty, I can't think when you do that." Hell, he couldn't get his hands to work in concert.

"'Kay." Kitty didn't look terrible worried about that.

"I want in you." He didn't want to come in her hand. Oh, he wouldn't mind it, but it would be better in.

"You want to use condoms? I'm on the pill, but..." She pinked. "I don't want to make you wigged."

"I'm good." He grinned at her. Just knowing that she had thought about it made it clear she wasn't the kind of girl who would take advantage, if that made any sense at all.

She popped the end of his nose with one finger then climbed on board, wet curls teasing his dick. Christ, she was nuclear hot. He could wallow in her, which was sexier than it sounded.

When his cock slipped between her folds, he had to grit his teeth to keep from going off like a rocket.

She was hell on his body and his sanity. Ace breathed deeply, his hands clenched on her hips, his jaw set. He could wait. He could.

"You're so fucking hot, Ace." The words were whispered, the sound almost filthy and exactly right as his hips slammed up.

He thrust deep inside and she closed around him, and Ace had to move. He couldn't give her time to adjust. *Fuck.*

"Yes." Her nails dug into his shoulders, driving in deep enough that they stung. "Again."

"Yeah. Kitty." He gritted the words out, and he was proud he'd been able to say that much. Then he plowed into her. He toppled them over, cradling her head until it was on the cot, then he went to town, needing nothing more than he needed this.

The bed rocked, but it held, thank God. They moved together like they were made to, like they could do this forever.

She was a wildcat, humping and moving, riding his cock. When his lips found her nipple again, he felt it everywhere.

Ace tried to ride it out, but the last little flutter of her muscles had him shouting, his cock jerking. He came hard, calling her name over and over.

Kitty shivered for him, moaning his name when she finally relaxed.

He chuckled, kissing her nose. "Sleep, darlin'. You're safe now."

Kitty hummed, then nodded. "Okay. Okay." She twined her fingers with his then sighed softly. "Okay."

Bless her heart, she was asleep before he took his next breath, her body lax and easy against his. She was plumb wore out.

Damn it, it would be so much smarter not to get involved with her. Too bad he wasn't very smart, because now Ace wasn't sure how he was gonna let her go.

* * * *

Ace snored. Not too loud and not terribly annoying, but he did and Kitty loved that she knew that. She'd missed it the first time they'd been together, but in her apartment she'd watched him for a bit while he slept.

It was still dark when she woke up, but she could hear the ocean, hear the waves on the sand, hear the rain patter against the tent.

It was the perfect way to wake up.

Ace shifted, snuffling, and his butt wiggled. God, that was adorable, so Kitty reached out, hand sliding over his ass.

"Hmm?" He shifted again, his muscles tightening.

"Shhh. You're okay. It's just me."

"You okay, darlin'?" Ace reached out, searching for her.

"I am. Watching the sun come up." She slipped closer, moving under his arm.

"Good." He hugged her close, his body warm in the cool ocean morning. "I like to go watch and swim sometimes."

"Yeah? Are you a water baby?"

"I was on the swim team." Ace chuckled, his back and ribs moving. "Don't let my height fool you."

"I never do. Show me?" She had a one-piece swimsuit in her duffel bag.

"You know it." He grinned and kissed her, lingering on it. It was nice, just a good morning hello.

Kitty kissed him back before she rolled out of the cot, kneeling down to find her suit. He got up and stretched, and even though it was still dark she could see how fine he was, how lean and strong.

She caught herself humming, appreciating the look, the view, even as she stepped into the black tank.

"You ready?" Ace pulled out a pair of trunks and slid them on, completely unselfconscious.

She slid the straps into place on her shoulders, made sure the leg elastic was right, and headed for him.

"You like to swim, darlin'?"

"I don't ever get to, but I like to. I run. A lot."

"I bet. That's the easiest way when you travel, huh?" He took her hand, pulling her down on the beach. "Lucky for me, most places I go have a pool."

"Do you have a pool at your ranch?"

"Yeah. Yeah, I put one in after I won my second championship." He wasn't bragging. He measured a lot by his career. She could relate.

"That's cool. One day I hope for an actual bathtub."

"I don't think you have room, darlin'." The water began to lap at their toes.

She laughed, the sensation tickling her. "Not yet, I don't."

"You should come to the ranch. Room I have."

"I'd love to see it." Her fingers twined with his as they headed deeper into the ocean.

"Excellent. Then you'll come sometime soon. You have to watch the undertow here." He kept her steady when her feet tried to go.

He was solid as a rock, and Kitty didn't doubt his strength for a second.

"You want to swim for real?" he teased, his teeth flashing in the gradual light of dawn.

"Yeah. Don't let me get lost."

"No. No, I'll stay close."

They struck out, and she could tell he was holding back to keep her there with him. She really wanted to see him go, though, see how good he was.

"Go ahead. Swim. I'm okay."

He was a dear man. A little voice in the back of her head whispered that he was clear enough that he didn't want to be worried about her job, and thus he didn't want to get serious. This was a booty call, pure and simple.

He stopped and treaded water. They were just far enough out that her feet didn't touch, but that meant the undertow was actually weaker. She could go horizontal for a while. "You sure, darlin'?"

"I'm positive. Go do your thing. If I get tired, I'll head in."

"I'll be close enough to hear if you holler." He swam right to her, giving her a wet, salty little kiss. Then he struck out, swimming strongly.

She swam parallel to the shoreline, using her runner's muscles to propel her.

Ace swam out until he was barely a pinpoint on the horizon, but she could still hear his arms and legs hitting the water, so she knew what he meant by he'd be close enough to hear.

God, he was strong, for being a fairly small man.

He turned then, disappearing under the waves for a moment before popping up and slicing through the water in her direction.

She moved more slowly, getting tired, but not exhausted. After almost a week of basic captivity it felt amazing to stretch her muscles.

Ace caught up with her in no time, and they turned toward shore without a word. He paced her, his body moving in perfect time with hers.

"Good swim?" She was actually breathing a little hard, wearing down.

"It was," he answered. They hit the beach, and she could see his chest rising and falling as he walked it off a little. "Killer surf today."

"It felt amazing. You swim like a fish."

"I love it." He shook his head, water flying. "You're stronger than you look for being so tiny."

"I told you, I run. I can run a marathon, even." She'd done quite a few for charity, though she preferred 5K runs for that. They took less training and were way easier on the feet.

"That's cool. I'm not near as graceful on land." He took her hand and pulled her over to a large, flat rock that looked like maybe Ace's friend had put it there as a bench. It put them right at the edge of the water.

She landed in his lap, laughing as her feet dangled in the waves.

"Nice, huh? Lucky has a decent little set-up." He held her close, keeping the chill from settling in.

"It's perfect. Remote, simple, and you're here." *Shut up, Kitty.*

"I like it better now that you are." He squeezed a moment.

Kitty rested her head on his shoulder, the sun warming the sky up.

This day was starting out so much better than the last month. She couldn't even begin to think about how much better it was. Ace felt strong and fine and steady and she could hear his heartbeat.

"I could stay here for days." Her fingers traced the scars she was beginning to know by heart.

"Yeah? I'm here for damned near another three days." His touch moved up and down her back above the line of her suit.

"You want company?" A fuckbuddy? Swim partner?

"I do." His lips traveled across her cheek.

"Excellent." She turned and brought them together for a good morning kiss.

Ace kissed her deep and hard, his tongue thrusting into her mouth. He tasted like salt.

She turned so her legs wrapped around his waist, so she could get a taste.

His hands slid down her back, to cradle under her ass. They slipped and rubbed together until the salt on their skin started to…chafe.

She chuckled. "Tell me there's some sort of shower set-up, even if it's a bucket in a tree."

"There is. Better than that, but it is outside." Ace stood, taking her with him, carrying her back toward his tent.

Okay. That was hot. Amazingly caveman, but sexy.

"Here we go." He overshot the tent by about ten feet, setting her down next to a little camp shower that managed to seem luxurious for its surroundings.

"Oh, perfect." She tugged him in, closed the makeshift curtain around them, then pulled him down into another kiss.

He took it easily, hugging her close, so close she could feel the hot bulge in his trunks.

Kitty pressed against him, dancing them together, just a bit.

"Let's get this off." Ace tugged at her swimsuit, pulling it down off her arms.

She wriggled out of it, the wet material clinging to her skin.

It landed with a plop, and Ace's swim trunks went next, pooling around his feet.

She needed to touch him, so she did, fingers stroking the velvet soft skin of his shaft.

"Oh, God." He grunted for her, his hips rocking, his cock straining. He liked that.

She did it again, teeth on her bottom lip as she watched.

Ace jerked, jerking against her again. "Make me crazy."

"I should. It's only fair."

He made her stupid, wild.

Ace smiled, the expression pure male satisfaction. He slid one hand to her breast, cupping underneath, thumb on her nipple.

Her hand tightened and she stepped closer as the touch made her ache.

"Sweet lady. Gonna eat you up."

"Swear it?" That sounded like fun.

He chuckled before bending to nip at her neck.

She tried not to laugh too loud, not wanting to wake anybody.

"God, you taste..." He licked where he'd bitten. "Salty."

"That ocean water will do that, every time." She felt that tiny sting all along her body.

"Yeah? I've never had the opportunity to lick."

Oh, tease. "Never? That's a shame. I think you probably have an amazing mouth."

"Oh, I do. Just, who was I gonna lick here? Lucky?" He gave a shudder.

That had the laughter pouring out of her, her whole body shaking with it.

Ace laughed with her, clinging to her, leaning on her. God, it felt like he heard her, he got her.

"Will you two either get to defiling my shower or keep it down?"

Oh, God.

Her eyes went wide.

Ace went into another fit of laughter. "Go away, Lucky."

She pressed close to him, giggles shaking her.

"Going to take Leroy to the cantina and breakfast. You two...defile away."

"Thanks, man." Ace waited a moment, maybe to make sure Lucky was gone. Then he bent and kissed her like he meant it.

Oh.

Oh, hello.

Kitty wrapped her arms around his neck, attention completely caught.

His leg slid between hers, pressing against her, giving her some friction.

Oh.

She arched and started moving, fingertips digging in as she did. The sensation hit her deep in her belly, a heat that built and built.

"Hot for me." He wasn't a huge talker, she knew that from before, but damn, when he did talk it had impact.

"Yes. Want you."

"Now, huh?" He lifted her easily, urging her to wrap her legs around his waist.

"You're strong."

"You're worth the muscle strain." He was a little breathless, but not shaking or anything, so she thought it might be from laughing.

"Butthead. I'll coat you in Bengay. After."

"Stinky." His cock thrust at her, the head slipping inside her.

"Burny." She held on tight.

He laughed again, his hands under her ass, moving her up and down.

"Don't drop me."

"Not gonna." No, he seemed pretty solid. Rock-hard.

Kitty squeezed with her legs, driving herself faster, riding him.

He moaned, his hips moving, his legs planted solidly to hold them up. His muscles bunched and pulled, just like when he swam.

"Love how you feel inside me." She took every inch, then lifted up and bore back down.

"Me too." He huffed a little, his hands clenching on her skin so tight it stung.

Every stroke down, his cock nudged her clit, drove her a little higher.

They were alone now, too, no one to hear, so Ace was talking to her, telling her how pretty she was, how wet. He was stunning.

Her muscles were trembling and she was right there, so close.

His fingers slid against her from the back, feeling where they were joined. *God. Please.*

He found her clit and it didn't take anything before she was coming, shaking hard for him and crying out his name.

"Kitty. Oh, man." Ace shook, his muscles quivering as he shot inside her, but he stayed upright. Mostly solid.

He eased her down, supporting her when her knees were weak.

"Wow." She said that about him a lot.

"You know it, lady." He hugged her tight, the move so unexpectedly sweet it made her tear up a little.

She looked up, kissed his jaw.

"Ready for some breakfast? We can take over Lucky's kitchen." He grinned, his eye lines crinkling.

"Absolutely. We can invent food." She was so fucked.

So fucked when it came to her feelings for this man that she didn't have.

"Come on, darlin'." They ran from the shower to the tent to get dressed, laughing like kids, and she didn't have any idea how she was going to leave.

So terribly, terribly fucked.

Chapter Nine

Ace felt like a million bucks.

He and Kitty had napped and eaten and loved up on each other all morning and most of the day. It wasn't until Leroy came looking to talk news story footage and plans to get back to the world that Ace took himself off, giving them the tent. He headed to Lucky's cottage, hunting a beer.

Lucky leaned against his futon, all sprawled out, staring at him, eyebrows raised. He looked like an ad for one of them beachwear lines, all white-blond hair and blazing blue eyes.

"What?" Ace went to the kitchen, opening the little apartment fridge.

"I thought you was queer."

He blinked, turning to stare over his shoulder. "Thanks. Asshole." The old joke was getting older every day.

"What? It ain't no big thing, man. I just… She's pretty. Little bitty, though. Seems to be into you."

"She's amazing." Ace pulled out his beer, popping the top. "Has a dangerous job."

"Leroy was sayin'." Ice blue eyes stared at him. "You cool with that?"

"No." He grinned a little. Lucky was always the razor among them, the Four Horsemen. Always willing to ask the hard questions, cut to the heart of the matter. "But I'm in too deep now."

"Ah. Well, then. Good luck on that. She met your momma yet?"

"No. I'll get her to come to the ranch here soon." He studied Lucky critically. "You need to get back to the world more, man."

Lucky flipped him off with a lazy motion. The man had lost his wife Vicki damn near ten years ago and he'd gone away, gone native. Ace could maybe get it, but shit, it was sad.

"I mean it. You should come with me and Steele and Cash to Reno or something." Lucky was still a hit with the fans, at least by web searches and shit that Emmy gave him reports about.

"Not going to happen."

"No? Why not?" It was way safer to talk about Lucky than it was Kitty.

"Just not. How'd she like the guest room?"

"She was fine with it. She slept like the dead." Kitty was so cute when she was asleep.

"Cool. Y'all can honeymoon here."

"I'd rather go to Belize." He always teased Lucky about choosing Mexico.

"Snob." Lucky grinned at him, winked.

"Nah. Not really." He took his beer to the futon, bumping shoulders with Lucky. It had been too long since they'd hung out. "I like it here."

"Yeah, it's a decent place." Lucky stretched hard, joints popping. "You know you're always welcome. Her, too. I mean, once you've made her legal and all." He got a shit-eating grin. "You know I don't approve of premarital fucking."

"That's because you're a freak—I don't buy a pair of boots without trying them on." Lucky had fucked everything that moved before he'd met Vicki. "I'm going to have to ease her into the idea of forever. I've been all non-committal."

"That actually sounds like fun." *Evil son of a bitch.*

"You suck. You gonna be in the wedding? She's bound to make Leroy be the maid of honor." That thought tickled him to no end.

"Dude, can you see that huge son of a bitch in a dress?" Lucky looked horrified. "Did you know he used to play pro football?"

"No shit? Who for?" He could see it. Leroy was a monster of a man.

"Coupla teams up north. Not the Cowboys." Lucky was a little one-minded when it came to ball games. Texas would always be king.

"Well, cool." God, was he really talking about marrying this woman? That was crazy, right? Just yesterday he'd been all freaked out about her job, but he did tend to make up his mind about shit and then do it.

"You want shrimp tonight? I was thinking about buying a bunch."

"That sounds great. We could do a boil, yeah? On the beach?" That would be fun as hell.

"You know it. A fire, music. It'll be a blast."

"Yeah." Ace clapped Lucky on the back. "You really think I'm the marrying kind?"

"Well…assuming you're not going to jump Silva's ass…"

"Balta? He's very busy." Ace wrinkled his nose, not wanting to think about that kind of busy. "Promise me you'll think about coming to an event. Even something small. Cash would love to see you."

Lucky shrugged. "I'll think about it. Cash knows where I am."

"He does, but he's really got his breeding program going good. Bulls are a hell of a lot of work." Ace peered out the door toward the tent, where Kitty and Leroy were deep in discussion. "Wanna play a video game?"

"Fuck, yeah. *Call of Duty*?"

"Works for me." Sometimes a man needed to let things go and shoot shit with his friends. He would worry about what to do about falling in love with Kitty later.

* * * *

If she never saw a man eat another shrimp as long as she lived it would be too soon.

Kitty had watched them pounce on the shrimp like a horde of ravening locusts. She'd even taken pictures for Honey, because that woman rode Leroy about cholesterol.

There were shells, butter sauce, tails and chewed corn cobs everywhere.

Talk about war zone.

Jesus.

Ace tipped back the last of his most recent beer bottle and grinned over at her. "Get enough to eat?"

"Absolutely." Leroy belched and she glared at him. "Don't make me call your wife, Big Daddy."

"What?" He gave her the innocent face, which never worked on a man his size.

She kicked him right in the ankle. Hard. "Butthead."

"Ow!"

Ace and Lucky cracked up, their laughter uproarious. She started giggling, chuckling into her hands. Then

Leroy broke up, too, wailing with laughter. They cackled until they were all wheezing, until her tummy hurt. Ace grabbed her around the waist, dragged her onto his lap, fingers tickling her ribs.

Oh, God. She was gonna pee. She knew it. Lucky was howling, slapping his leg, just rolling. Ace was all hands, making her squeal.

"Ace! Uncle!" She got a stitch from laughing so hard.

"I don't know, guys, can she call uncle?" He stopped tickling, though, just holding on.

Leroy nodded. "I reckon she can, man. Although I bet you aren't feeling much like her uncle right now."

Oh, evil turd!

"No, sir." Ace grinned down at her. "Not that I'll discuss it with you, Leroy."

"Good answer." She kissed his chin.

"I thought so." Ace glanced around at Lucky and Leroy. "Guess we need to clean up, guys. I'm pooped."

"Man, that's the worst part."

Lucky grinned over. "We could play a round of cards, loser cleans."

"That works for me." Ace bounced her a little. "You play Spades?"

"Yeah, actually." She could play almost any card game and lose or win, depending on what the situation called for.

"Cool."

Lucky nodded. "A true test of a new couple. Can they partner?"

She chuckled. "We'll see how I do. Ace may decide to beat me."

"That might be fun."

Ace kicked Lucky, which made them all chuckle again. Then they were digging in and getting the cards out.

It took them all a hand to remember how to play, then they needed a few hands for everybody to get a feel of it. Then Leroy bid nillo and the game was on.

Lucky had the most amazing hand, and she and Ace went down in flames for at least three go-rounds before they caught a break and bid eight and made it. *Damn. Good game.*

Ace was easy to partner with, and they laughed together, teasing hard.

They ended up neck and neck at the last hand, and Leroy went nillo. It was as if Lucky could read Big Daddy's mind, because they pulled it off.

In the end, they all cleaned up though, Leroy carrying trash to the burn barrel, Lucky emptying the huge pot from the boil.

Ace was a good loser, scrubbing bowls and cups, helping put the card table away.

Leroy and Lucky grabbed the last couple of beers when they were done, and Ace took her hand.

"Come on, darlin'. Time to let the boys bullshit." He winked, waving goodnight to the others.

"And what are we going to do, Ace?" She thought bullshitting was not on their menu.

"I think we're gonna go hunker down and get to know each other even better."

"Ooh. That sounds like fun."

"I think so." His hand felt warm around hers, a little rough.

"We could play twenty questions."

"You think so?" Ace snorted, climbing into the platform tent with her. "What do you want to know?"

She was a reporter. "Everything. What's your favorite cereal?"

"Lucky Charms. What do you like to read?"

"For fun? I love spy novels from the Eighties." She winked, and they settled together. "What's your perfect Saturday morning?"

"When I'm working, it's when everything goes as right as it can. When I'm not, it involves pancakes." His fingers slid into her hair, pulling the strands apart.

That made her smile. Pancakes were her specialty. "You have the best hands."

"Yeah?" He grinned down at her, his smile lines amazing. "I like your boobs."

She rolled her eyes at him, but beamed. No one had ever said that to her. Ever.

"What? I do." He slid his hands down over her shoulders and arms.

"No one's ever said that to me." She slipped into his lap.

"No?" He rubbed noses with her even as he started working at her button-down shirt. She'd worn it over her bathing suit. "It's true."

"That's incredibly hot." And she felt like a million bucks.

"So are you, darlin'." Her shirt went the way of the dodo, then the straps of her swimsuit.

Her nipples were hard as nails, already aching just from how he looked at her.

"Look at you." He lifted her breasts, his thumbs rubbing her.

"Ace." She moaned, teeth sinking into her bottom lip. *Oh, God. So hot.*

"Kiss me, darlin'." He bent to her mouth, licking at her lips, making the bottom one sting where she'd bitten.

His fingers kept moving, tugging a little then flicking, and she moaned into his mouth. He was too good at that. Ace moaned, too, driving toward her, his hips rocking.

He was hard for her, she could feel it through his swim trunks.

His skin was on fire for her, his body moving sharply now, caught in the dance.

He was going to make her come, just like this, from rubbing and touching and petting her.

Maybe that was okay. Ace sure seemed to think it worked, the way he kissed her as if there was nothing else he wanted to do.

She rolled and cried out, her belly tight against his.

"God. Kitty. I love your skin." He stroked her side, her hip, loving on her.

Her entire body blushed, pleasure heating her, core deep.

Ace was focused. Starting to get demanding, maybe, his touches more firm.

She nodded, panted, her thighs damp.

"How am I doing so far?" He kissed her throat and it took her a moment to remember them teasing about what they would do when they got back to the tent.

"I. Good. So good." She was going to shake into a thousand pieces.

"Glad to hear it, darlin'." He was a magic man, touching her all over.

"Ace..." She needed more, needed a little more.

"I got you, Kitty." He so did. In the palm of his hand. He touched her where she needed it most, his fingers working her clit.

She arched over him, fingers digging into his shoulders, the waves of pleasure hitting her so hard that she couldn't breathe, could only nod and move.

Ace was staring at her, loving her with his hands. He was something else, something special.

"Oh. Oh. Ace..." She lost her words and settled for moaning low as she came apart at the seams.

"God, darlin'." Ace moaned a little, his breath coming hard and fast.

She swooped down, took his lips, kissing him with everything she had in her.

Opening up, Ace let her take his mouth, his body pressing close. His skin felt so damn right.

"Want to ride." She groaned the words into his mouth. She was so ready and she wanted his cock.

"Oh, hell yes." He rolled them so she could climb on top.

She spread, taking him in hand, sliding him over her folds.

"Come on, Kitty. You said you wanted me in." Now he was starting to look a little desperate.

"I do. I..." She lined him up and sank down.

"That's it." His eyes closed for moment then opened back up, focused on her.

"Love how you fit inside me."

"Me, too. Christ. Love how you feel." His jaw clenched, his body moving faster.

She added her own strength to the thrusts, riding him hard.

Ace grunted and suddenly they were racing toward the finish. She felt it in every line of his body.

She wanted to come too, again, whatever.

She moved faster, demanding.

Ace helped her out all over again, one hand sliding to her breasts, the other down between them to touch her.

"Good to me." *Yes. Yes, right there. Fuck.*

"I try, darlin'." He tried hard. He was holding back for her. Waiting.

It didn't take much, though. He tweaked her nipple, pulled almost too hard and she gasped, the zing of pleasure-pain sending her over.

Ace cried out, the sound all about need and completion. He felt heavy and right inside her, as if he fit.

She could feel him, deep. She held on tight, letting them both float down.

Ace stroked her back, loving on her with his fingers. His chest rose and fell hard.

"Thank you."

"Hell, thank you." Ace was grinning down at her, those amazing dimples appearing.

She chuckled, drew him down for a nice, long kiss.

Ace kissed her back, slow and thorough. He was warm and heavy, his breath slowing.

The way he looked at her, well. She thought maybe he loved her a little, too.

Hell, she could hope, couldn't she?

Chapter Ten

The mercado was tiny, but Kitty didn't seem to mind. Ace adored how she loved life, how every colorful piece of pottery or jewelry caught her eye like she was a tiny magpie.

Shit, he'd seen magpies bigger'n her in Colorado.

Her curly hair shone in the sun, her big shades hiding her eyes, and she was the prettiest thing he could ever remember seeing.

They stopped at a stall selling seafood stew of some kind with big pieces of fresh bread. "You want some, darlin'?"

"Absolutely." She kissed his cheek, laughing softly before heading to the elderly woman there and jabbering at her in Spanish. She'd eat anything, try anything. Hell, Lucky'd had her out on a damn surfboard, falling so many times she bruised and he'd had to growl.

They ended with two big Styrofoam cups of *sopa del mar* and two big chunks of bread that they took beneath a shady awning to eat standing up.

"Oh, man. Oh, man. Taste that. People in the city don't know what they're missing."

He watched her munch her way through a soft-shelled crab, admiring the sheer bravery that took. If she could do it, so could he.

Every so often she'd touch him—little, familiar touches that made him tight, made him want to rub all up in her business.

Him Tarzan. Her Jane. *Yum.* Ace wanted to drag her off to his cave.

The neat part was he was fairly sure she'd let him. Then she'd roll him over and hump him into oblivion.

"What are you thinking about?"

"Huh?" He glanced up from her boobs, hoping he didn't have sea legs dangling out of his mouth. "Having sex."

Kitty's laughter rang out, making people look over, smile.

"It's a thing when I'm around you." His cheeks heated but he had to grin. It was the truth.

"I like that...thing."

"I like how you like it." They were both going to go up in flames.

Her smile was pure sex, those pretty eyes making promises.

"Hey, *puta*, you still here?" Somebody clipped Kitty on the shoulder as he walked by, spinning her in place.

Ace caught her before she staggered, but then he took two long steps and caught the bastard by the arm. "Apologize to the lady, mister."

"*Chenga te.*" A knife came out of fucking nowhere. "You get less nosy *putas*, eh?"

"Back off, Jorge, or I'll call *Señor* and your ass is mine." Kitty was right there, eyes flashing.

Ace wasn't scared of a knife. This guy was a fucking coward if he picked on women. Ace moved between Kitty and Jorge. "Get your ass on out of here, boy."

One eyebrow arched. "Careful, *gringo*. A girl could get lost, in a place like this."

"You think so? I think a man could get his ass kicked by a *gringo*."

The guy brandished the knife, opening his mouth to say something else.

"Jorge!" Kitty shouted. "No!"

Ace, now, he was done with all the talking. He went in low and fast and the knife went spinning away.

He took one shot in the chin, but that was it, Leroy and Lucky showing up about the same time as about ten thousand of Jorge's closest friends did.

Ace and Lucky ended back to back and Leroy looked like something from some *Lucha libre* wrestling league, tossing Mexicans about like a bull flinging snot. It was a thing of beauty.

Then someone discharged a firearm and all of Jorge's friends disappeared like smoke.

Someone else grabbed Kitty's arm, tugged her off her feet and she twisted, kneeing the bastard in the groin. *"No me moleste!"*

Good girl. Ace sent the guy reeling with an uppercut, hauling Kitty up against his chest. "You okay?"

"Can we go now?"

"Yeah. You guys okay?" Lucky and Leroy were right there, Lucky grinning like a fool.

"Let's *hasta*, buddy." Lucky hooted. "Damned cowboys, messing things up in my new hometown."

"Yeah, yeah." Ace took Kitty back to Lucky's Jeep, all of them piling in. Damn, he'd been hoping for some sponge cake for dessert.

"I'm sorry." Kitty offered Lucky a weak grin.

"What for, honey?" Lucky chuckled. "They don't come near me. They think I got landmines on the beach to keep drug boats away."

Leroy looked back at her. "You okay, baby girl?"

Kitty nodded, lips tight.

Ace knew she was barely holding it together. He wasn't sure how he knew, but he did. "She's a trooper, Leroy. She surely is."

"She's a stud." The man's dark eyes held his gaze, deeply serious.

Ace nodded, so proud of her he could bust.

She was quiet the whole way to Lucky's, but there wasn't a single tear.

Ace kept a hand on her back, rubbing a little. He wanted to get her a drink and get her alone and just hug on her.

They parked the Jeep and Kitty slipped out, headed immediately down to the water. Leroy sighed and got out too.

"You okay, big guy?" Ace wanted to go after Kitty, but he wasn't going to interfere with Leroy and her if they had some sort of crisis ritual.

"That depends, son. You gonna go let her cry on you or do I need to, 'cause she's gonna and I ain't letting her do it alone."

"I've got her." He smiled and clapped Leroy on the shoulder. "You let Lucky see to your cheek. It's all cut."

"Good deal." He got a nod, a grin. The man was solid people.

Ace trotted down to the beach, hunting Kitty, who would burn to a crisp in the late afternoon sun.

He could see a bruise coming up on her arm, could see the way her breath hitched a little as she walked the edge of the water.

God, he wanted to go back and beat Jorge down. He wanted to kill the man for hurting her. Course he wanted to go to Kitty more, so he did. He wrapped his arms around her. "I got you, darlin'."

"I-I'm okay." She sniffled a little, then leaned hard.

"I know. Adrenaline." His hands shook a little, proving he wasn't immune.

"Yeah. Yeah. I'm sorry. Are you okay?"

"I'm fine, darlin'." He was right as rain. A little ragey, but fine. "Are you hurt?"

"Sore, a little. Nothing big." She was trembling against him.

He kissed her temple, smoothing her hair back off her face. "Okay. We could go soak a bit. Lucky says there's the best tidal pool up the beach from where we were last night."

"Yeah?" One tear slipped out, sliding right down her cheek.

"No swimming required. Just floating." He held her tight, letting her cry it out if she needed to do that first. Tears did the same thing to him as they did any cowboy.

Pure panic.

Still, she might need it.

The storm was quick and left her red-eyed and flushed but looking a little less wild. "Let's go. Suits optional?"

"Yep. No one here but Lucky and Leroy, and they'll be drinking beer and telling tall tales."

He wrapped an arm around her waist and led her to the beach.

Her cheek ended up on his arm as they walked.

Better.

Ace sighed a little, relief making him kinda lightheaded. So much adrenaline, he figured. Still, when they got to the hip-wader and got naked, that went away real quick. Kitty had that effect on his thing, after all.

* * * *

She woke up early, every inch of her sore — some from the fight, some from the wild sex — and headed for the little outside grill, hoping to start both fire and coffee.

It was quiet, Ace sleeping back at the tent, and she could so see why Lucky had squatted where he did. The ocean seemed vast, the whole world kind of shiny and new.

The grill was already going, though, the little percolator popping away.

"Morning." Lucky came from the direction of the shower, wearing only a pair of low-slung jeans.

"Hey." She smiled, waved a little. "How's it going?"

Lucky was a beautiful man. Not like her Ace, but pretty like wow. Her Ace was...pure, unadulterated sex in boots.

"Good." He had a bruise on his jaw that she hadn't seen from a distance, covered as it was with blond stubble. "You okay? Want some coffee?"

"Please on the coffee. I'm fine. Sorry about yesterday." She knew Lucky was the one who had to live here, after all.

"No problem, honey." He winked. "I meant it about the landmines."

"This is a great place." Lucky arched an eyebrow at her and Kitty shrugged. People assumed things about her because she lived in the city.

"I like it all right. I mean, it's not like Ace's ranch, or Steele's big spread." Lucky shrugged.

She chuckled. "I have a four hundred square foot apartment. I love it."

"Lord." He shook his head. "My bedroom was bigger than that as a kid. You'll have to move in with Ace. He'll never go the other way."

Right, because Ace was looking for permanent. "Mr. Porter has already explained that he's not interested in that sort of relationship. He's fine with me in the city. This was just…a happy accident."

If Lucky's eyebrow climbed anymore he would lose it in his hair. "Huh. He calls you darlin', Kitty."

"He does. I call him Ace." Although she was considering Studmuffin—that would make him laugh.

Lucky gave her a long look. "Well, let me tell you, lady. I've heard him call women all sorts of things. But his daddy called his momma darlin', and he's never used it on a girl before."

Her cheeks heated, and her heart pitter-patted a little bit before she gave herself the firm lecture about Ace being smart enough to know what he wanted. And what he didn't want. And he didn't want a woman who worked in a dangerous job. "I understand, but he's been very clear about things. He's not interested in someone like me, not in anything long-term. It's a sweet thought though."

"Sweet." Lucky hooted. "Yeah. I'm sticky sweet like wet sugar. Here, honey." He handed her a cup of coffee. "Sugar and all is right there. How do you feel about French toast?"

"I think it's absolutely wonderful." Breakfast food of any sort was on her yummy list.

"Cool." He grasped her shoulder for a moment with a coffee-warm hand. "Don't rule him out yet, honey. Never think a Horseman is out of the race."

She surprised herself by tearing up. *Jesus.* "I'll crack eggs for you, if you want."

"Sure thing, honey." He grinned, squeezing before reaching down to pat her butt. "I got good Mexican vanilla."

"Be nice. One cowboy is more than any woman can handle."

"Oh, I'm out of the game." There was something dark there for a moment, something in those pretty blue eyes that looked a lot like devastation. Then he grinned again and they got to making breakfast.

That was a shame, too. Ace had told her that Lucky had lost his wife years ago and was still missing her terribly. It broke her heart, a little.

"So, have you been to Ace's ranch? Y'all should go there next." Sausages went on the grill, sizzling some.

"I haven't. He seems to love it, though." This friend of Ace's didn't seem to get 'not involved'.

"He does. It's got a sweet practice arena." Lucky laughed, the sound husky and sweet. "He should put you on a mechanical bull."

"I'd try it." She was up for anything.

"Try what?" Ace's hands slid around her waist from behind, his lips pressing against her neck.

"Good morning." She hummed softly and leaned. "A mechanical bull."

God, she loved the way his scent surrounded her. That was one reason she'd fallen for him.

"Oh." She could feel the little electric jolt that went from him to her. "I'd like that."

She couldn't help her chuckle. "Then you'll have to show me how."

"I can surely do that."

She'd seen video of Ace when he was riding, on YouTube and on the league website, but she'd never seen it in person.

Lucky's chuckle was filthy, knowing, and she glared at him. "Aren't you supposed to be cooking?"

"Me? Cooking. See?" He started dipping bread, whistling.

Ace glanced back and forth between them. "Has he been working his Lucky charms on you?"

"Nope, but he did make me coffee." She turned to give him a hug, a good morning kiss.

He kissed her back, nice and thorough.

Oh.

Good day to her.

Ace made her dizzy, made her reckless, and she loved it.

He squeezed her ass for a moment, then patted it. "Did you say there was coffee?"

"I did." She stepped away and went to pour him a cup—black.

"Thanks, darlin'. You need any help, Luck?"

Lucky shook his head. "I got this. Y'all should go have your morning swim or smoochies or whatever."

Her cheeks heated but she handed the coffee over, followed that fine butt wherever Ace led.

Ace chuckled as they walked, sipping his coffee. "Lucky hates to admit he's a hopeless romantic."

"How long since he lost his wife?"

"Just over six years. He retired early, came down here."

"That's awful. I'm sorry." She rested her cheek against his shoulder.

"He's done all right. We miss him some, you know?" Ace's even breathing made her head rise and fall, just a little.

"Yeah. I understand that."

She let her fingers rub his lower back.

He hummed for her, holding on, hugging on her.

"I'm glad I ran into you, Ace."

"So am I, darlin'." He kissed her, soft and warm and good morning again, and she thought he meant it. She really did.

Chapter Eleven

Kitty landed in DFW in the International Terminal. It had been a vicious flight from Dubai, especially since Leroy had left her at Heathrow, heading for Houston. She probably should have just traveled with him, but she hadn't seen Ace in nine weeks and, damn it, she wanted to. He'd told her he'd thought he could get some time off, and she'd given him her flight information, let him know that she'd get a hotel room somewhere close once she arrived. She didn't want to expect him to come for her, or even let her stay at his place for the ten days she had before she was due in Houston, because what if she was wrong and disappointed? She wanted some face time.

All she had to do was rent a car and not fall asleep before she drove west.

She watched the luggage spin on the carousel, blinking grit from her eyes. She had no idea what time it was, but it had to be an off time, because baggage in the International Terminal was deserted, only the people from her flight on this whole aisle. Well, them and one Wrangler-wearing cowboy, who was headed her way.

She blinked, rubbed the bridge of her nose as the tears threatened. *Oh, please God. Please, let it be Ace.*

When the man got close, she saw those unmistakable dimples, that scar, even if Ace's eyes were shaded by the hat, pulled down low. He reached for her, his arms wide open, and she went right into them.

"Hey, darlin'."

"Ace." She kissed his jaw and held on. Tight.

"No bags yet?"

"Not yet. Thank you for coming out."

His hand stroked through her hair, petting her and relaxing her.

"I wasn't gonna make you go to a hotel, darlin'. I missed you." He kissed her temple.

"Missed you. How's work?" The baggage carousel buzzer rang and the belt started moving.

"Busy as a one-legged butt kicker." He grinned. "We got a bye week coming up, though, so I'm off for six or seven days. Troy and Sandy can hold it down."

"Oh, that's excellent timing." She grabbed her first bag, hunting for her second.

"It is." He took the bag from her, grinning a little at her raised brow. "It's in my genes."

She made a show of looking below the belt. "I have a thing for your jeans, Mr. Porter."

His grin widened and something started poking against the fabric of his jeans. She liked that, too. "That it?" he asked, pointing to the matching bag that was coming around.

"It is." She let him grab it, then took his elbow when he offered it. "Thank you."

"My truck is a ways out. Do you want to wait at the loading area or come on with me?" His hip bumped hers.

"I'll come with you. I've been sitting for hours."

"Sounds good to me. You up for stopping to get a bite to eat? I'm starving." The air was hot and muggy, but after Dubai it seemed almost cool.

"God, yes. Airplane food is… Well, you know, yeah?"

"I do. Where were you again?" Sometimes Ace had a little trouble with geography. At least outside of Texas.

"India, then Dubai City." She tried to smile. "It's beautiful, but…I'm really glad to be home."

"I'm glad, too." He shook his head. "I thought I traveled a lot. Man, that one time I had to go to Australia I thought my ass would fall off."

"Did you like it there?" She explored his arm, the little scars there on the skin.

"It was pretty. Everyone talked like Packer Stevens." His skin drew up with goosebumps under her touch. She could feel them.

"Dubai was culture shock-y the first time, but I've traveled there a ton. It's easier now. I got fabulous footage." God, she wanted him.

"Cool. I missed you fierce." He grinned sideways at her, pointing out a big dualie. "There she is."

"Oh, wow. Look how pretty!" Huge and dark blue and shiny — it was a beautiful truck.

"Thanks. It does what I need it to, huh?" He hit the unlock button and put her bags in the back seat, then helped her into the passenger side.

She leaned down, kissed his cheek, ducking the hat brim.

Ace put one hand behind her head and pulled her down for a real kiss, his head tilted just right so she escaped a brim bashing. *Oh, hello.*

Oh. Oh, God. He made her wet faster than any man ever had. She leaned against him, tongue sliding against his, tasting him.

They pulled apart, panting, when someone honked at them, shouting out the window as the big SUV went by. Ace smiled, wry and apologetic. "Sorry, darlin'. I got a little lost."

"I understand." She blinked, chuckled softly.

"That's what I want to hear." He kissed her lightly once more before tucking her into the truck and closing the door.

"It smells like you in here." She leaned back, surrounded by goodness.

"Does it?" He got them going, muscling into DFW traffic like it was nothing. Maybe for his truck it was.

"Mmhmm." She reached out, fingers tracing the seam of Ace's jeans.

"Now, woman, you watch that." He laughed, but she could see his muscles jump.

"I am, Ace. I promise."

He laughed harder, shaking his head. "You get to me so fast. I swear it's magic."

"It's amazing chemistry. What are you hungry for?"

"I could go for some barbeque. What do you think?"

"Anything but curry or cabrito."

"No. No curry." His face wrinkled up.

She giggled. "No? I've had…a lot. A lot a lot."

"I imagine. I might die." Traffic finally started to thin out a little and Ace put the radio on.

"No dying." Her eyelids got heavy and she watched the lights go by.

"We could get takeout, darlin'. If you're sleepy."

"No. No, I'm okay, just a little jet-lagged. I don't even know what day it is, for sure."

"Uh." He blinked. "Me either."

She started laughing, tickled, and so happy to have her cowboy. "No? We're a pair!"

"Yeah. I don't work, I have no idea." Ace reached down to hold her hand. "I think we make a great pair, darlin'."

Oh.

Oh, damn.

She was too tired to not let that hit her, square in the heart. Kitty closed her eyes to fight the little prickle of tears, and when she woke they were out of anything that looked city-like. She'd been more tired than she thought.

"Oh. I'm sorry. I dozed off."

Look at the stars.

"No problem. We're only about twenty minutes from the ranch, and I know the best barbecue place." They were back in a town, not a big city.

"Excellent." Kitty sat up, stretched. "I'm terrible company, huh?"

"Nah. Now you can be awake enough to keep me company when we get to the ranch. That's way more important." His dimple drew up on his cheek, his sideways glance evil.

"Listen to you flirt. I approve."

"Well, I hope so." He patted her leg, which was not quite asleep. When he pulled into a barbecue place called Outlaws, she was ready to move a little.

"Oh, that's a happy-making smell." She pulled down the visor, flipped up the vanity mirror. "Do I look okay?"

"You look amazing. I could have you for dessert." Ace hopped out and came around to open her door. "Of course, they have amazing peach cobbler."

She chuckled, let him help her down. The tiny little things like that made her smile, made her happy.

Tucking her arm into his, he led her inside, where it was all neon and smoked meat.

Everyone seemed to know him, and some recognized her, with that odd blink and twist of the head. Ace didn't seem to be bothered, so Kitty shrugged it off too, and let him lead her to a little table for two.

She settled in, ordered a Coke, and took one of the rolls they brought over.

Ace grinned. "So, what was the best part of Dubai?"

"We didn't see much. I was interviewing a man who helps dissidents leave China." She explained how they'd been picked up as soon as they'd hit the ground, blindfolded and taken on a six-hour trip to God knew where.

It had been a wild trip.

"Ah. Well, damn, if I'd known you liked blindfolds…"

She looked at Ace, genteelly flipped him off.

He chuckled, grabbing her hand across the table. "Now, is that any way to treat a man who's going to introduce you to the best barbecue ever?"

"I suppose — if it's really the best…" They laughed together, fingers twining.

"It's pretty darned good." Ace ordered them a little of everything, it seemed, from brisket to turkey to sausage.

"Has the season been going well?" She was trying to learn about bull riding, rodeo, doing her research in her off time.

"Yes and no. There were a lot of injuries last season, and a lot of our best have been sitting out." He shrugged. "Course that means we've got some great rookies."

"That's handy, I guess. Are your rookies new to the sport or just to your..." She reached for the word. Team? League? Club? "Organization?"

"They're new to the big league. Kind of like baseball." The food came, and it did smell mouthwatering.

"So you started the league with Lucky?"

Oh, smoked turkey. Yum.

"Yeah. And Cash and Steele and Troy. We were all working rodeos and thinking we could make more money." He handed her the bowl of potato salad.

"Thank you." She nibbled on the potato salad. "I've met Troy — older gentleman? A little round?"

"Yeah. He was a generation before us, really. He's the old man." Ace was packing away the food — for such a relatively small man, he could eat.

"He was dear." And the only one of them all who had recognized her from the news.

Ace hooted, slapping the table. "I'll have to tell the boys. Troy is terrifying to the guys on tour."

"Troy? Really? I thought he was sweet."

"He likes you. He told me he watches your show religiously."

She grinned, pleased down deep. "I like to hear that. There's so much competition." Especially with the male reporters. They aged so much better.

"He's tickled to death. So is his wife."

She arched an eyebrow. "She a journalism fan?"

"She's more a 'let's get Ace settled' kind of girl." His cheeks pinked, the flush going to his ears.

"Oh." She wasn't sure what to say to that. Not at all. "Well, I'm glad you were still available, when we met."

There. That was non-committal enough, right?

"So am I, darlin'." He gave her that slow, hot grin, and all she could do for a moment was stare.

Sipping her Coke, she let her legs rub together. She'd thought she was too tired to pounce Ace, but it seemed like she was wrong. That nap had been restorative as hell.

Ace looked pretty happy to be with her, too, which warmed her heart. He paid at least as much attention to her as he did his cobbler.

"Do you want me to get a hotel room for my visit, or…?"

"Whut? No. I told you." His head whipped up and he stared. "No, darlin', I want you in my bed."

"Oh, excellent." Kitty nodded, ignoring that rejoicing little voice inside her. "I want you. I want to spend this time with you."

Maybe she needed to.

"Well, then." Ace nodded, like that was that, and waved the waitress over. "Can I get a box for the leftovers, Char?"

"Absolutely, Ace honey. You want a little extra for the dogs?"

"Please, ma'am. How's your granny?" Ace chatted to everyone who came by, which was so weird for someone who'd lived in New York as long as she had. She sat quietly and listened.

She learned all about Charlene's granny, about Mr. Doc's bad leg and about Ollie Andersson's dog, who'd had a litter of thirteen.

It occurred to her that she didn't know what kind of dogs Ace had, how many there were. She didn't know what his favorite football team was, or if he liked chocolate chip cookies. She knew his birthday was Christmas Eve, though, and what he weighed, how tall he was, his stats from his last active season.

Hopefully she could find out a lot more this weekend.

Ace looked at her suddenly, snapping her out of her thoughts. "You all ready?"

"I am. I am. What kind of dogs do you have?"

"I have two border collies and a heeler. My momma has two Bluetick hounds that pretty much live at my ranch."

"Are they big?" Not that she was scared of dogs or anything, she just...didn't know any.

"The hounds are the biggest. Rosie will love you. She's the best herder I have." He grinned, and she liked how happy his dogs made him.

They headed out hand in hand. "I've never had a dog."

"No? I grew up with a whole pack." He handed her up into the truck.

"My parents aren't animal people." Her parents were very...clean.

"Oh, God. You're in for a shock. I got cows, horses, dogs, barn cats... I think old Dave might even have an emu."

"Oh, how fun is that?"

"Emus? They're vicious, darlin'." They headed out of town again, where there was lots of open space.

"Are they? Why?"

"Heck if I know. Birds are smart, I guess."

"I guess. I got bitten by a parrot on assignment once." She'd had a bruise for weeks.

"Birds are evil, darlin'." He put a hand on her leg, stroking lightly.

"Mmhmm..." She felt goosebumps rising over her arms.

"Not much longer now. You can rest up some. We can have dessert."

Yeah, his touch was soothing. *Ha.* "The stars are amazing out here."

"They are, huh? I'm always amazed when we go someplace and you cain't even see them."

She loved the way he said 'cain't'.

"Just huge. It's better than the city lights." *Almost.*

"Well, hopefully you won't find it too quiet at night or nothin'." They turned up a side road and bumped over a cattle guard. She'd learned about those in Argentina. Fascinating how cattle wouldn't step over them at all.

They pulled up maybe five minutes later at a house, a solid-looking ranch-style place. Pretty. At least what she could see from the porch light that was on.

He pulled all the way to the steps, the headlights showing a porch swing for two, roses, a front door with a huge glass star in the front.

"Here we go, darlin'." His accent got deeper with every inch closer to the house. He hopped out and came to get her, grabbing her bag.

"It's lovely." The air was heavy, humid, the sound of the buzzing floodlight surprisingly loud.

There were other sounds, like insects and maybe cows and all, but they were soon drowned out by the baying and barking of dogs. "They don't bite, right?"

"Nope. Y'all settle down." Ace patted heads and scratched ears and the dogs sniffed her.

She petted and patted, chuckling as whiskers tickled her. They were curious, but well-behaved, and only two came inside with them, a fuzzy black and white and a hound.

"You want a drink, darlin'? Need to call anyone?" He was hovering close, shoulder brushing hers.

"No, Ace." No, that wasn't what she needed at all.

"Well, then…" He grinned at her, his hand sliding down her arm so his fingers could twine with hers.

She found herself standing there, grinning back.

"Come on." He tugged, and she got the short tour of the house, from the big designer kitchen that had to be his mom's influence to the bedroom, with an amazing king bed and a wall of windows.

"Oh, look at this. Decadent." She walked over to the bed, hand trailing along the comforter.

"You like it? I added on the whole thing when I made my first championship." He sounded so tickled.

"I love it. Your bed's bigger than my whole apartment."

"Yeah, I guess it is at that." *Look at those dimples.* "Come over here."

When she got near enough, he kissed her, his hands on her shoulders to hold her close.

Loved him. She *loved* him.

She tamped that little voice down, got it quiet.

Ace pulled her to the bed, sitting and getting her situated on his lap. He seemed pretty happy to have her there, so take that, little voice.

"Hey. Happy..." What day was it? She still didn't know. "Tuesday?"

"Very happy. Been missing you, darlin'. Bad." He nuzzled under her ear, breathing deeply.

"Ace..." She shivered, nipples going tight. "I want you."

"Good. I want you, too." His hands found her breasts, lifting them under her shirt.

Her eyelids got all heavy, her hips starting to move almost immediately.

"Such a pretty lady." He watched her intently, his thumbs pressing her nipples. She moaned, leaned into his hands. God, she loved his fingers—callused and rough and perfect on her skin. "You feel like nothing else. Hot, soft. Perfect."

"You've got amazing hands."

"I try, darlin'." He started working on her clothes, getting her bare.

She would have covered her breasts when he pulled the shirt off, but he moaned, eyes on her as if she was everything he'd ever wished for.

"I swear, you're enough to make a man crazy." He touched her like she was precious, like she was perfect.

"Only want to make you crazy." And she needed him to make her crazy.

"Well, you got me, lock, stock and barrel." Ace tugged her jeans off in one smooth motion.

Her little black lace panties went next—they never had a chance. They sailed away and Ace lifted her, kissing her again, letting her feel him.

It felt incredibly naughty to rub against Ace, her naked body against his clothes.

It felt even better when Ace lifted her higher, licking his way down her neck.

"Ace." Her nipples were like rocks, tight, tense, taut.

He nibbled at her skin as if she was the best kind of feast. She started making hungry, needy sounds. She couldn't help herself, and Ace wasn't doing much better, his sounds more like grunts and clicks. Very caveman. Incredibly hot.

She approved.

He finally tossed her onto his bed. She wasn't sure she knew they'd moved. She slid her hand down her belly, her body aching already. "You have too many clothes on."

"Do I?" He glanced down, actually seeming surprised. "Damn."

"Lose them." Her eyes ate him up, wanting to see every beautiful, scarred, tanned inch.

"You got it." Ace started shucking clothes, his eagerness flattering.

"Good man." She loved how he looked—every muscle tight and compact, body built for efficiency. His belly was flat as a board, the six-pack barely defined, not all bodybuilder. His legs were fuzzy and strong and built to hold on.

She sat up, reaching for him, needing to feel him, how warm he was.

Ace came to her easily, his hands sliding up her arms, her hands landing on his chest. He was burning for her.

"You make me want things, Ace. Everything." She rubbed her cheek on his belly, breathing him in.

"You feel amazing, darlin'. Been missing you." He stroked her hair, his hands slipping through the heavy stuff over and over.

It almost made her teary, but she held back. She wasn't going to ruin this.

He kissed her so deeply then that she forgot to worry about crying. It was as if he wanted to eat her up. That worked for her. It really, really did. One hand wrapped around her thigh, dragging her leg up, spreading her for him.

"So pretty. So wet, darlin'. Are you ready for me?"

"Yes. Yes, we'll take our time later."

"Hell, yes. I've got to check every inch and make sure it's okay."

She nodded, grabbed his hot, heavy erection and guided it into her.

"Oh, fuck, Kitty." Ace gritted his teeth, his whole body shaking for her as he slid home. He filled her up, cock pressing the walls of her cunt, stretching her. He was on fire inside her, his skin hot against her breasts and belly as he moved in and out.

"Ace. Ace, so good." She held on tight, fingers digging into his upper arms.

Panting, he nodded, his eyes bright, almost feverish, gold instead of simply hazel.

His hips rolled, giving her clit almost enough pressure, almost enough friction. Almost. She wrapped her legs around the backs of his thighs, tugging. It worked, because he slammed into her, rubbing hard.

"There!" *Yes. Yes.*

"I— Oh, damn, Kitty." He kept moving, hard and deep.

She was going to scream with it, her abs so tight they burned as her need flared.

"Kitty. Please. God." His jaw clenched, his hand sliding beneath her to move her faster.

"Need. Ace. Oh, fuck." The filthy word pushed out of her.

"That's it." His dimples flashed, his smile as dirty and fun and all that. He bent then, his mouth on her breast.

Her orgasm hit her hard and she arched under him, that tug on her nipple like being hit by lightning.

"Fuck. Kitty." He was barely making words, the sounds guttural, as he moved hard and fast.

"Yes." That was the best she could do.

Ace slammed into her one last time, his head snapping back, his body shaking.

"Fine." Ace was so fine, needy and strong, and he made her ache.

"My girl." He rubbed noses with her when he sank down on her.

Ace's girl. *Damn. Yes.*

She took another lazy kiss.

He held her close, loving on her with his hands and his mouth, slow and easy.

"Missed you, Ace." God, she was tired. Fading. Jet lag and good food conspired against her.

"Can't say I'm sorry you're here and in my bed, darlin'. I've got you. Sleep." He stroked her back, the touch sweet.

Sleep.

She could do that.

* * * *

Ace woke up with a crick in his neck, one arm asleep and the need to pee pressing at him pretty damned hard. He was also smiling. Had to mean Kitty was right there in his bed.

She was sleeping hard, too, cuddled into his side, lips open against his skin.

God, she was beautiful. He was... Well, he was a goner, was what he was. He wanted to keep her.

He brushed her hair off her face and those pretty-pretty eyes blinked open, her smile sweet as hell. "Morning."

"Hey, darlin'. Get some decent sleep?" She'd been so damned tired.

"I did. You have a comfortable bed."

"I like it." Everyone who'd seen it teased him that it was too big for his little ole body, but Ace didn't care. It was a fine bed.

She nodded. "Me too." Her stretch rubbed her soft skin all along him.

Damn, he loved how she felt next to him. "Want to do breakfast here?"

"Mmhmm. I do. You have to show me around."

"Oh, there's a lot to see. I'll show it all to you, though." He grinned, his hand sliding on her ass. She cuddled into him, fitting like a hand in a glove. He stroked her back, his fingers counting the bumps of her spine. Sweet lady. His. "You'll have to meet all the hands, too."

"I've already met both your hands, Ace. I'm a good, good friend."

Ace blinked then chuckled, smacking her butt just hard enough to make a noise. "Turkey."

"Gobble gobble gobble." God, she made him laugh.

"I could gobble you up. Better feed you first, huh?"

She could freshen up while he cooked.

"Sounds like a plan. Where's your bathroom?"

"Just through there." He nodded toward the en suite, then headed off to get some sweats on and get breakfast going.

She came out as he was putting sausage in the pan, hair in a towel, his robe wrapped around her. "I borrowed this, I hope that's okay."

"It looks good on you." Shit. What had he been doing?

"It smells like you." She went to the coffee cups he'd set out on the counter.

Ace grinned. She was obsessed with how he smelled. "Well, I guess that means Steele hasn't been using his spare key and bringing women here." That was a stupid thing to say. She'd addled his brain.

He got a raised eyebrow look. "You should tell him he ought to keep a spare here for that. God knows where people have been and robes seem pretty personal."

"They do." He shook his head. "It was a bad joke." He hoped.

She chuckled, came to him. "It still smells like you for sure, not someone else."

"And it looks good on you." He'd said it, but it bore repeating.

She leaned against his chest then offered her lips for a kiss.

Ace took it, and took his time, too, exploring her mouth fully. She was so much better than eggs.

Her hands moved on him, fingers touching and stroking.

"Gonna distract me, darlin'." He was already pretty distracted.

"Yeah." She untied the robe, the move easy and sensual as all get-out.

Ace stared down at her, taking in her small, perfect breasts, her tiny waist and surprisingly lush little ass. Fuck, he was a goner. A sweet blush started climbing her body, her nipples tightening up, just from him looking.

He loved that, loved how she reacted to him. She was something else. She was his. *Damn it.*

He'd tried hard to make himself keep it light, but it wasn't.

It wasn't light, damn it.

He kissed her to keep himself from saying anything stupid, shoving his tongue into her mouth.

Kitty arched, nipples sliding on his chest as she opened to him.

Ace grunted, the feeling so fucking overwhelming, that he wanted it to keep on forever. Damn it all, he needed to let it go and love on her.

"Ace." God, she wanted him so much.

"I got you, darlin'." He kissed her again, hands on her ass.

She bucked into his touch, rocked toward him.

They broke for air finally, and Ace stared down at her. "Did I turn everything off?"

"You did." She took his hand, put it on her soft, wet pussy.

"Oh, good." He put his other arm around her, lifting her up on the table.

The robe parted, the sun touching her pale skin. God, he could eat her up.

He eased her back, stepping between her legs. He was aching to be inside her, so he shoved his sweats down.

"Ace." She spread for him like warm butter, just giving it up.

"Kitty. So pretty." She looked...what was that word? Wanton? He'd never really understood that till now.

Course nobody'd ever looked at him like he was the finest thing she'd ever seen.

She made him feel tall as mountains, which was silly, 'cause he was a shrimp. Still, he wanted everything from her. Now.

The tip of his cock nudged her folds, slipped against her.

They both sighed, and Ace slid up and forward, sliding inside her. Perfect. She was perfect.

Her smile was the prettiest thing he'd ever seen.

Words that he wasn't ready to say sprang to his lips, so he bit down on his lower one, letting his body do what it needed to.

This was the easy part, filling her up, feeling her and making her fly. He'd never known a woman so responsive, so eager for every little sensation.

Ace moved, back and forth, sliding in so easy, pulling back with effort.

Her hands kept moving on him, on her, driving things that much higher.

He chanted her name, panting, sweat pouring off him. He wasn't gonna make it much longer.

Her fingers slipped down her belly, sliding down to where they were joined and Ace could feel her hug his cock.

"Fuck." The word burst out of him, his body trembling like a leaf.

She nodded, lips parting as she moaned for him.

Ace lost control, moving harder, faster, his balls so tight they might explode. He was so ready.

He felt it when she came, shuddering around him, moaning his name.

"Oh, Kitty." He shook for her, his hips bucking hard. God, he was so hot for her.

"Yes. Filling me up."

"Yeah. I swear, you're gonna be the death of me." He couldn't half breathe.

"Drama queen. Fuck me." Her eyes twinkled, the tease damn near evil.

"Thought I did." Ace just cracked up.

They laughed together, and damn, it felt right. Perverse, but right.

Ace thought he might could do this for a long while. Good thing she had some time off.

He cupped one of her hips in his hand. "You ready for breakfast, darlin'?"

"Sounds perfect."

"It does." He was relieved that he'd turned the stove off so nothing burned.

"It'll all be fine." He wasn't sure if she was talking about them or the food.

One way or the other, he hoped to hell she was right.

* * * *

Kitty stood on the front porch, looking out into the vast amount of land all around. It amazed her, how…empty the view was without buildings.

It was stark and hot and fascinating.

Truly fascinating.

Ace had gone to another part of the ranch to speak to his mother. Kitty had decided to stay, see the dogs, check her email. Rest.

It felt awesome to be utterly out of her own skin, her own world. Like it helped her let go.

She went to put on her bikini, found a spot in the backyard, and stretched out under the sun on a low chaise.

She had a tussle with the dogs for a few moments, but they got bored pretty fast and headed off, sniffing things like dogs did. The only sounds were birds, leaves rustling on the couple of big trees and the occasional bray of a donkey. Which made her laugh.

The sun beat down on her, made her all boneless and lazy and sleepy.

She had no idea how long she soaked in the sun, but she knew it when something cold and wet landed on her belly.

She squealed and sat up, grabbing her untied bikini top as she did.

"You're gonna burn, darlin'." Ace grinned, waggling the bottle of sunblock at her.

"You squirted goo on me!" And it was sliding.

"So I could rub it in." Ace squatted, easing her down on her back.

"Okay then. That's acceptable."

"I thought it might be." One of his hands landed on her belly.

Her bikini top slipped, only the barest bit.

Ace stared a little. He was such a boy.

"I was avoiding tan lines."

That was an acceptable explanation, right?

"Sure." He wasn't blinking. At all. Only staring.

"It's cool, right? To sunbathe topless out here?" She let it slip a little more.

"Yeah. I mean, the hands don't usually come up here, and Momma is off doing whatever."

"Okay. Then I can do this?" It was down to her nipples.

"You can knock yourself out, darlin'." Ace reached up from her belly, tugging the top all the way down.

"You'll have to put lotion on them."

"I will." Those slick, callused hands slid up her ribcage, to cover her breasts.

"Oh…" Her eyes rolled and she moaned, nipples tightening at the touch.

He pressed his thumbs against the tight buds. "I swear, you ever change these and I'll beat you."

"I…" *Okay, wow.* That was both chauvinistic and hot. She knew that her breasts weren't perfect, but to hear that… He made her melt.

He was so absorbed in her skin that he missed her blinky reaction. Probably a good thing.

His fingers plucked her nipples, tugged a little, and she moaned, legs shifting. She was wet, just like that, and thank God he'd said no one came out here. They would be putting on a show. He did it again, then again, before letting go. Her body followed his touch, shoulders lifting off the chair.

"Better?" He was hoarse, his eyes hotter than the sun beating down.

"Uh-uh. I think." She swallowed. "I think you rubbed all the sunscreen off."

"You think? I can try again." Ace pulled the bottle up and squirted more into his hand.

"I think that's safest." Kitty needed his hands on her.

"Oh, safety first, darlin'." Ace laughed and rubbed her some more.

She held the moans for as long as she could, but her nipples tingled, ached, the tug making her feel like there was a string between clit and breasts.

Finally he bent to kiss her mouth, his hand sliding down to rest against her belly again.

She kissed him like her life depended on it, as if she could shove him over and ride him into the ground.

Oh, yummy idea.

Ace grunted when he landed on the chaise, blinking at her. "Kitty?"

"Yeah?" She tugged at his buckle. She wanted his perfect cock.

"Well, now. You're gonna have to be careful not to let that get too much sun."

"Swear, it won't get burned."

"Fabulous. You'll cover it up, huh?" He chuckled, reaching for her. He still had too many clothes on though.

"I will." She slipped her bikini bottoms off, got his jeans down past his hips.

"Hoo, yeah." He lifted her, pulling her over his pelvis.

"Want your cock, Ace. Want you to make me come." It was really exciting, to be the wild one.

"I can do that, darlin'." He grinned up, his eyes glinting, and he dove between her legs.

They fit together so well, and she rocked back, taking him. "God, yes."

His hands were on her hips, tight enough to leave marks in her skin. He moved her up and down, up and down.

Kitty was right where she wanted to be, head thrown back, throat working.

Hot. He was so hot, and the sun made her skin tingle. It felt so good, so amazing.

Her hands were on his chest, grabbing his T-shirt as she moved, his cock filling her up.

One of his hands finally shifted, first to pinch at one nipple, then down to slide between them. He found the spot where they joined, then moved up a fraction, his fingers finding her clit.

"Oh." Her entire body lit up, her hips moving faster.

"Fuck, darlin'. So good. More." Ace was rocking, touching her like she was his and only his.

She'd never been so wild for a man, so needy.

He braced his feet against the ground and thrust into her, slamming against her butt.

Kitty's eyes went wide, her orgasm hitting her like a runaway freight train.

Ace grunted, his head falling back against the lounge. He came hard for her, his throat working, tendons standing out.

"H...hey." Sweat slid down her breast, one drop beading at the nipple.

"Hey, darlin'." Ace looked absolutely debauched. It was a grand thing.

"Your little cowboy butt will burn, if we're not careful." God, he was hot.

"It's not my butt I'm worried about." He grinned wider, rubbing his hands over her torso.

"I have that other part covered." She leaned into him.

"You need to not burn you. That's important."

Oh.

Oh, so sweet.

"You helped with that." He made her a little stupid with the sweet things he said, with his country manners.

"I need to do your back." He pulled her down to lay on his chest, his hands gliding over her back.

God, he was...

Perfect.

Well, except for that whole 'I don't want to tie myself down' thing.

That was kind of a bummer. Not that she'd gone into this whole thing with him wanting to jump into something serious.

She didn't need serious.

Permanent.

She wasn't looking for anything more than this.

Right?

Right.

Then why did she want nothing more than to lean down and snuggle into Ace's arms and stay?

* * * *

Ace loved grilling meat. He loved it, from starting the fire to the smell once the burgers or steaks were on the grill.

Tonight he was doing steaks and shrimp. Kitty was sitting on the deck with her bikini top and a pair of cutoffs on, and she looked fine enough that he was worried about burning the meat.

She was painting her toenails and laughing at the dogs, who were in the yard playing.

"So, where did you grow up again, darlin'?" He knew she was from the Mid-West-ish, but he knew very little about her, really.

"Outside Kansas City. Far enough out that it was smallish, but not remote."

"You never did have dogs, did you?" She seemed to like his well enough, which was handy.

"Nope. Mom and Dad were OCD. My aunt had one name Tippy."

Ace chuckled. He thought maybe everyone had a Tippy in their life at one point or another.

"I haven't seen anyone in a long time. Leroy and Honey are my family."

"You're going there soon, huh?" He liked Leroy, but hadn't met Honey.

"For my birthday."

"They live down in Houston, right?"

She nodded. "They're having a big barbeque thing for me, Honey's making me a carrot cake."

"I love carrot cake." Not that he was begging to go or anything. Not at all.

"Yeah? Are you...I mean, it's nothing big, but... If you want to come, I love to have you there."

"Yeah?" Ace tried to match her casual tone, but he was all-in now. "I could drive you down."

Kitty grinned at him, a real, full-on happy smile. "Yeah? I. I can't think of anything I'd like better."

"Oh, cool. I'd love that." He so would. Just to spend more time with her.

She stretched out, wiggling bright pink toes. "Me too."

"Cool." He turned the steaks, careful not to squash them down against the grill. He didn't want the juices to escape.

"Can we go swimming after supper?"

"Absolutely." He loved Kitty and water. He'd thought of her every time he'd gone swimming since Mexico.

"Cool." She stretched, moving under the sunlight, her skin barely glowing.

"Yeah." Fat dripped down into the flames and Ace jumped at the sizzle. God, he was a fool for her. He was addicted to every part of her little body, from her upturned nose to the little scar next to her bellybutton.

Ace swallowed hard. Steaks. He had to get the grilling done.

"Son, I brought you some peach cobbler." *Damn. Momma.*

Well, at least they weren't naked. "Hey, Momma. We were just fixing to have steak. You want me to toss something on for you?"

"No, son. Minnie and LuAnne and me are going to Linda Harper's." Momma's dark eyes landed on Kitty, sharp as tacks. "I came to meet your lady friend."

Kitty stood, graceful as you please, and smiled at Momma. "Ms. Porter, I'm Kitty Carpenter. I'm pleased."

Momma's lips twitched. "Aren't you a Katherine?"

Kitty chuckled. "Only professionally."

"Well, I like it. I'm Carol." They shook hands and Ace breathed a sigh of relief.

"It's nice to meet you." Kitty grabbed a black T-shirt and tugged it on.

"You, too. You like cobbler?"

"I love cobbler. Love it." Kitty grinned. "It's the absolute taste of summer."

"Well, then, be sure Ace shares with you."

"Don't worry, Momma. We share well."

Kitty's face never even twitched, but Momma's eyes caught him. "Impertinent."

"You raised me. You ought to know." He went to his momma and kissed her cheek. "Thank you for the dessert."

"You're welcome. Would y'all like to come out to lunch tomorrow?"

He glanced at Kitty, who smiled and nodded. "Sure. About one?"

"Perfect. You bring the beer." Momma kissed him again. "I'll be out late. Don't worry."

"I won't. Minnie is a superior designated driver." He patted her butt, which made her whap him, laughing all the way through the house when she left.

Kitty chuckled. "She's fierce."

"She's nosy." He winked, pulling the steaks off.

"I can understand that."

"Yeah. Sorry about that, darlin'." Mainly he was sorry she'd put her shirt on.

"I wanted to meet her. Who knows what fascinating secrets she can tell me?"

"Oh, man." He'd have to watch them at lunch.

"Something's on fire." She grinned at him, eyes laughing at him.

"Shit!" He'd forgotten the corn, one ear of which was in flames.

Kitty came up behind him, helping out with the hot pad in hand.

"Thanks, darlin'." He smiled at her, just happy to be with her.

Her laughter chased him to the grill. He rescued supper, happy to sit with her and eat, maybe watch her a little. She was so damned fine, sitting on his deck.

The sun lit her up, especially now that the T-shirt was gone, letting him see all that skin.

He reached over, cupping the ball of her shoulder, his thumb sliding on her skin. It wasn't sexual, really. He needed to feel her.

She leaned over, kissed his hand, the motion easy as pie.

Ace felt his smile stretch his damned cheeks. She made him damned silly. He might have to consider keeping her just like he did every minute of the day.

Chapter Twelve

They pulled up to Leroy and Honey's house mid-afternoon, the huge sprawling ranch as familiar as her own place. "This is it. "

They'd had a great drive — coffee and breakfast at the start, barbeque for lunch. Music and laughter and silly stories.

Kitty was so far head over heels she couldn't bear it.

"Nice." Ace sounded genuinely pleased, which made her smile widen. Oh, yeah. Ace was becoming her world.

She nodded, opening the truck door as the twins barreled out of the house. "Aunt Kitty!"

"Boys!" She opened her arms for the kids, the ten year olds taller than her now.

They tumbled over her, laughing, talking all at once. They could make a din.

Cassie and Elmond — the teenagers — came out more slowly, Cassie with baby Bella in her arms.

"Hey, Aunt Kitty." They both peered curiously at Ace.

"Hey, guys. This is Ace Porter, my friend. Ace, this is Cassie, Elmond, Bella, Mark and Mike."

"Hey, y'all." Ace nodded and grinned. "Where do I put the presents?"

"Momma's got a table for them. Aunt Cissy is coming, so are Rita and Matt." Cassie smiled at Ace. "Elmond will carry suitcases. He's trying to get into JV football."

"Well, then." Ace started chatting football with Elmond, handing off bags. It was cute.

Cassie came close, handing her baby Bella, who settled against Kitty's chest like a dream. "So is this him? Mr. Cowboy Man."

Kitty nodded. "Yeah. He's…mine."

"He's okay. A little pale."

"He's a nice man." Cassie had no idea.

"Cool. Come on. There's food." There was always food at Honey's.

"Kitty-Kat!" Honey came out the front door, a force of hips and bright patterns and boobs and a stunning smile.

She was enveloped in a huge hug, then Honey stepped aside to look Ace over.

"Honey, Ace. Ace, this is the best cook on earth, Miss Honey."

"Baby girl!" Leroy's voice boomed out. "Happy birthday!"

Ace nodded and held out a hand to Honey while Leroy came to give her an embrace that swallowed her whole. God, it was marvelous to see him.

Honey pulled Ace into a hug as Leroy tugged Kitty inside. The huge old place was decorated for the party, the smell of fried chicken on the air. Home.

It felt incredible to be home.

"Did you have a good break, baby girl?"

"I did. I swam and tanned and goofed off. You?"

"I ate." Leroy patted his belly. "Luckily, Honey worked me out."

"Cleaning the attic?" she teased.

"Garage." Honey kissed her cheek, grabbed Bella. "And the storage building. He was a good man."

"There was some more personal stuff, too."

Honey pinked and laughed and Kitty chuckled. Leroy was more in love than any man she'd ever known. It was fabulous.

"Hey, Leroy." Ace grinned and held out a hand to Leroy. "Pleased to see you again."

"Ace, man. Fucking glad you could make it."

"Leroy!"

"Daddy!" The twins stared. "Daddy has to put money in the swear jar!"

Kitty felt her eyebrow arch impossibly. "Swear jar?"

Honey nodded. "Mike got detention for cursing at school."

Leroy sighed. "My fault, or so I'm told."

"Absolutely. Curse words have never crossed my lips." Honey's eyes were dancing.

Ace nodded solemnly. "It's always Kitty."

"Oh, you turd!" She whacked him on the butt. Hard.

Ace jumped a mile, laughing like a loon, and Honey cackled. "The quiet ones surprise you. Come on, y'all."

The kitchen smelled like heaven and she put Ace's beer in the fridge. "I'm going to show Ace where to put the bags, okay?"

Honey nodded. "Good deal. You're in your same room."

She spent a lot of time in the guest room, enough that the kids called it Kitty's.

"Thanks."

She smiled and Ace took the bags from Elmond. They headed down the hall to the bedroom, which was hers, not just a guest bed.

"This is mine, mostly. When I stay here."

"It's nice." Ace nudged her with an elbow. "A little frilly."

"I'm a girl." She winked, chuckled. "Honey spoiled me."

"Doesn't look a thing like your place." He grinned back. "Do I get to stay in here?"

"So long as we don't make a deal of it, yeah." She thought, anyway.

"Cool. I wouldn't do that in front of your family." He smiled, bending to kiss her cheek.

"I know."

That was the best thing about Ace. He respected her, even if he did act like a cowboy some of the time, especially about her job and her boobs.

He hugged her hard. "So, I bet they're waiting. Come on, darlin'."

She nodded and took his hand, leading him downstairs to the people who she was the closest to in the whole world.

Leroy was waiting with another hug. "Guess what?"

"What?" She leaned into him, grinning at Honey.

"Honey is making fried chicken."

"Oh. My. God." She let her knees buckle dramatically. "I should go running now to save calories."

Honey cackled and Leroy looked mournful. "Running. God help me."

"Because you're so fat, Kitty." Cassie came up and goosed her. "You're a size what? Double zero?"

"She's small but mighty," Ace agreed, giving her a wink.

"The camera doesn't forgive. I've talked to your dad about that a hundred times and he still makes me look bigger than I am."

Leroy snorted. "Good thing I'm behind the camera, then, huh? Come on. I want to get a game of Spades in before supper."

"Ooh. You remember how to play Spades, Ace?" They'd played at the beach but had all needed a refresher.

"I do."

"Excellent. Ace is on my team!"

Leroy's hands clapped over his heart. "You wound me!"

"She just loves to see us play partners." Honey smiled so sweetly that it boded ill for Leroy.

"I'll be Honey's partner after Ace and I kick your butt."

"There you go! You don't mind, do you, buddy?"

Ace clapped his hands. "Nope. I am an equal opportunity ass-kicker."

"Bad word!"

The kids hooted and Honey pointed to the swear jar. "Mr. Porter."

"How much does that cost?" Ace dug out his wallet, laughing good-naturedly.

"A dollar."

Her eyes landed on him. God, she loved him. The thought made her shiver, but she did. Silly as it was, she loved Ace Porter.

"Oh. Well, here's ten, just in case." He stuffed a ten dollar bill in the jar.

Then he grinned at her, almost as if he knew what she was thinking.

Leroy patted Ace on the shoulder. "Come on, man. Help me get the table set up."

Ace went and she headed to get a glass of water and to ask if Honey wanted help. She figured Honey would say no—she was a disaster around boiling oil—but she asked anyway.

Honey handed her a bowl of greens when she walked in. "Make sure there's no grit, will you? He seems nice. Pale, but nice."

"He's amazing." She blushed and headed to the sink.

"Oh, now. Look at that." Honey chuckled, the sound low and a little ribald. "You got a thing."

"Hush. You hush. It's a one-way thing, okay? He's not as into me as I am him. He's never said the L-word."

"Seriously?" Honey looked at her a long moment. "He doesn't have the look."

She shrugged. "There's history, I think. Girls trying to push too hard. It doesn't matter. I'm a city girl that travels nine months a year. He's a rodeo cowboy that travels nine months a year. We're made for flings."

"Well…" Honey frowned, lips pursing up. "We'll see."

"Quit worrying, Mom." She winked over.

"Hey, someone has to worry about you." Honey whapped her butt.

She snorted, splashing Honey with her fingers. "Yes, ma'am. I believe I have cards to beat you at."

"You do. The rest of supper can wait until it's time to cook. Just let those soak."

She nodded, then went over to get a hug. "Thank you."

Honey kissed her cheek. "Happy birthday, Kitty

They really were her family. It made her happy to be there with them.

Leroy hollered from the game room then, and she and Honey headed off to battle.

She was taking no prisoners.

* * * *

Ace owed the cuss jar eight more bucks by the end of the night—Honey and Kitty had routed him and Leroy in the card games they'd played after supper. The ladies had been out for blood.

Still, Honey made the best fried chicken on earth, and Kitty looked so tickled when the kids brought out the cake and presents.

He figured that the party meant family, not a bunch of folks.

Kitty seemed about as relaxed as he'd ever seen her, laughing and barefoot, her hair in a ponytail.

"I made your card!" Ace couldn't for the life of him remember the kids' names, but one of the little ones was waving an envelope.

"Oh, did you?" Kitty opened her arms then scooped the little boy up and let him tell her all about it, her blonde head next to his dark one.

"I did." He chattered and she opened the card, *oohing* and *ahhing*. She was damned handy with kids.

He could see it, actually, her with a baby. It was a satisfying thought, a primal one that hit him deep. Really deep. Like balls deep, and suddenly he was glad he was sitting down.

He felt eyes on him, turned to see Honey smile at him, and he found himself blushing.

Lord. There he was, wool-gathering about babies. He had a present for Kitty, but he wasn't gonna give it to her with Honey watching him like that.

Kitty glanced up at him, smiled and winked. "Having a good time?"

"I am. You like your cards?"

"I love them."

She leaned back, stretching. "Tell me we don't have to go back to work in a week, Leroy."

"I'd tell you, baby girl, but I would be lying."

"Oh. I hate Mexico City."

"Mexico?" Ace gave her a hard stare. "Why are you going to Mexico?"

"Work." She sighed. "We've got a guy willing to talk to us about the latest cartel killings, if we meet him."

"I told them the same thing I see in your eyes, Ace." Honey gave him a warm pat on the arm. "Didn't they have enough trouble last time?"

Ace nodded. "That was exactly what I was thinking."

"It's a big story."

Leroy nodded. "We ever want to get something bigger, we got to hit these hard ones."

Kitty chuckled. "Yeah, and a boob job. No anchor jobs without the B-cup."

Ace put his hands on the table and leaned in. "No boob jobs."

"That's what it takes, to get the anchor job."

No. No way.

Those pretty breasts were perfect. Perfect and sensitive as any woman he'd ever met.

"Well, then, you'll have to settle on something else." He said it easy, winked, but he meant it. He knew it was her body and all, her decision, but he couldn't see her changing it for a job.

No way he was losing the way his girl moaned when he used his mouth on those pink, hard nipples. No way.

Honey and Leroy were staring at him—Leroy looked shocked, but Honey was grinning ear to ear.

He grinned, too. If she made anchor, Leroy would lose his job. He'd have to mention it at one point.

Kitty rolled her eyes, snorted. "I think we should do an exposé on the bull riding league, Leroy. How they're hiding all the cowboys left in the world and trampling them with cows."

"Sure." Ace nodded easily. "I have it on good authority of my webmaster that we should get a documentary done."

Leroy chuckled. "I think that your objectivity is a little off there, baby girl."

"*Moi*? Personally biased?" Kitty's eyes went wide and they all cracked up.

Honey and Leroy waited for the kids to drift off before giving Kitty her gifts. They knew her well, giving her Kindle cards and travel shit.

"Thank you." She gave them both kisses. "You're good to me."

Leroy chuckled. "You're family, baby girl."

It was telling to Ace that Kitty came to Houston for her birthday, not to New York with her friends there. Course, at least Houston was in Texas.

And before she'd come here, she'd come to him. He grinned a little, knowing he probably looked like an idiot.

Kitty settled beside him, leaned a little bit, let him feel her softness. "Having a decent time, Ace?"

"Better than. I got something for you, too, darlin'." He'd gotten it at the jeweler in town while Kitty and his momma had gone to the Brookshires.

"You did?" She blushed so pretty. "I didn't expect you to…"

"Well, I know, but I wanted to give you something pretty." He pulled the little flat jewelry box out of his pocket, hoping to hell it was appropriate. He'd gotten her a little gold St. Christopher medallion on a chain that seemed delicate enough, but that Gary the goldsmith assured him would hold up in the field.

She unwrapped it, fingers moving over the pendant. "Oh, Ace… Look how delicate."

She held the box out to him. "Put it on me?"

"Surely." He undid the wee clasp and slid the chain around her neck, smoothing it into place once he got it closed again.

"Oh, sweetie… Look at that."

Kitty got up and showed it off to Honey and Leroy, then came back to him and gave him a soft kiss. "I love it. Thank you."

"You're welcome, darlin'." It glowed against her skin, which was tanned to a light gold. She probably wouldn't get darker than that if she wasn't brown after a week at his place out by the pool.

Look at her.

Damn.

His girl.

He blinked a couple of times, trying to keep from kind of overflowing with joy right then and there.

She kissed the corner of his mouth again, then settled. "What a great birthday."

"Yeah? I'm glad." He put an arm around her and squeezed, happy to be right where he was.

Her cheek found its spot on his shoulder as Leroy found them a movie to watch.

It was definitely like being with family, and he could appreciate it. Right until he dozed off.

The movie was off and the room was dark when Kitty's lips brushed his temple. "Ace? Love? Let's go to bed."

"Hmm? Oh. 'Kay." He grunted, climbing to his feet and helping her up.

She led him upstairs, handed him his ditty bag and pointed him toward the bathroom.

Ace stumbled to the restroom, passing her going there on the way back. He felt a little more awake, though, so he changed into his sleep pants and waited for her.

She slipped back in the room wearing one of his T-shirts and a little pair of panties, her hair back in a ponytail. Oh, God. He'd been thinking about just going to sleep...

She climbed into bed next to him, soft and sweet-smelling and still wearing his necklace.

"Good birthday, huh?" He reached for her, holding her close.

"The best." She kissed him, body fitting against his like a dream.

Ace smoothed his hands up and down her back, the soft T-shirt material not near as nice as her skin.

"Love your hands." She smiled at him, legs twined with his.

"Yeah?" They were catching on the material a little, the calluses heavy.

"Yeah." She wriggled, tugged the T-shirt up so he had skin to touch.

He stifled a little moan, touching her like he wanted, sliding his hand up her belly. Those sensitive nipples were waiting for him and he took his time getting there, counting her ribs, teasing her skin. "Perfect. Could eat you up, sweet girl."

"What?" The right nipple went rock hard.

"You heard me. These are perfect." He used his free hand to pull her T-shirt up under her arms. Damn, he loved how she smelled—powder and apples and something else. Something amazing. He bent and nuzzled the top of one breast, teasing both of them.

"Ace." Her voice was husky, soft, and she was starting to shift, shiver for him.

"Love your skin. Love the way you shake for me." He licked at her nipple, teasing it back and forth as she strained toward his lips, that needy bit of flesh hot as a brand.

He groaned, sucking some, really letting her feel it. Her fingers tangled in his hair, little sounds catching in her throat.

"Darlin'. Taste so fine." He kissed and licked then started across her chest to scale the other little peak.

"You make me crazy." Breathless and gasping, she sounded like a wet dream, and when he pressed his thigh between her legs, she started shifting like she was riding.

"Good. Want you as crazy as I am." He moved her thigh up to give her more friction, his cock tenting in his sweats. God, she was hot against him, rubbing nice and steady.

He needed to get those panties gone. His sweats, too. Had to. His amazing girl must've read his mind, because she got his cock free, got his bare thigh against her. Now he needed to get those little lacy panties off.

Ace grinned a little, his fingers finding the string of the string bikini and breaking it. Ta-da.

"Ace!" She popped him on the nose, giggling softly.

"What? This way we don't have to wiggle too much." He kissed her to stop the laughter that bubbled up.

He shoved the material aside, let her wet lips kiss his thigh. God, that felt incredible. He'd done that to her, and it made him hard as a rock.

She moaned deep in her chest when he cupped her breast again, fingers teasing one hard nipple.

He kissed her hard, opening her mouth with his, and he twisted his fingers the tiniest bit. That made her roll against him, curls sliding on his cock, sweet as fuck.

Ace tried to breathe, tried to stifle his noises. This wasn't his house.

"Please. Please, Ace. Want to come."

"Okay, darlin'. Okay." He wanted to come too, so he arched and slid his cock against her folds, seeking entry. He sank into her, balls deep, loving the soft little sound she made for him. She was hot, slick, and she fit him so well he knew he was home.

"Yes." Her lips were on his jaw, trailing over his skin.

"Faster, Kitty. We need to move faster."

"Faster..." She shoved him over, straddled him and started to ride, bouncing on his cock.

Ace moaned low, his hands on her ass, his hips rising and falling. Damn, but she could ride. He watched every second, even when his eyes wanted to close with the pleasure of it.

He reached down, his fingers sliding between her legs, finding her clit. He needed her with him when he came.

"Ace." She arched up, her pretty lips parting.

"Come on, darlin'. Show me." He kissed her again, his lips pressing to hers a little desperately. He felt it, all around his dick, as she let go, came for him so pretty. Ace gritted his teeth, his body bucking, his hips slamming up. He came so hard it almost blew the top of his head off.

"Oh, man..." Her lips brushed his shoulder, his collarbone.

"Was I loud?" He sure didn't want Leroy and Honey kicking him out.

"Don't think so." She kissed his cheek.

"Oh, good." Ace chuckled. "Happy birthday."

"The best one yet." She rested down on him, heavy and soft.

She snuggled right in, and Ace let his eyelids droop. He even liked her chosen family. He hoped she liked the rest of his as much.

Chapter Thirteen

God, Kitty didn't want to go to Mexico. She was so tired of traveling and she wanted, of all things, to go back to Ace's ranch and hide.

"That was a big sigh, Kitty-Kat," Honey told her. "Why so gusty?"

"I'm wanting things I can't have." Ace had gone back to work, driving out of Houston late the night before. Kitty had a bit of a reprieve, the contact in Mexico needing two more weeks before he could get away into the city to meet with them.

So, she was working with Leroy for a few days on footage, then going to New York for a meeting or two with execs.

Right now, though, she and Honey were making chocolate chip cookies. She reached up to touch the St. Christopher medallion around her neck. At least she always had a bit of Ace with her.

"You know, you said he's not the hanging around type, but that cowboy is in love with you."

She glanced at Honey, hope leaping in her chest. "Do you think so? I've never been so deep with someone. Not even Miles." And she'd been engaged to him.

"I know it. I see how he looks at you, though. He's in love. I know it and I ain't never wrong."

Honey was a dear, trying to reassure her. Kitty just felt as though she and Ace were in different orbits, and she couldn't figure out how to make them coincide.

"Well, I sure hope so. Nuts now?"

"Yep. Then we get the scoops." Baby Bella began to cry, and Honey went to the carrier propped on the counter to grab her. "She's hungry. Do you mind if I…"

"No, go ahead." She wasn't afraid of breastfeeding. The sight of Honey and the baby did make her a little teary, though, thinking about a baby with Ace. Oh, God, where had that come from? She had a job. Ace didn't want a baby right now, or to be tied down.

She blinked rapidly and began scooping out cookies and plopping them on the parchment-lined cookie sheet. Ace would love these.

Stop! You're an emotional mess. No more Ace, she told herself firmly. Not for five minutes, at least. Then she could pine all she wanted.

Surely she could manage five minutes.

* * * *

"So you're not in Mexico yet?" Ace waved off one of the interns, knowing he had to get back out there and finish the details soon, because the show began in forty-five. God knew today had been a clusterfuck from the start, from Empire State having an injured hoof to one of the bullfighters, Nate, ending up stuck in Montana and not being able to make the performance.

Kitty calling was the best thing that had happened to him in days.

"No. We had a delay. I know you're tickled," she teased.

"I am. I admit I hate that you run into danger for a living, but if anyone can get an unbelievable story out of it, you can." He was trying for supportive. He really was, because it wasn't fair to use her work like a sword to dangle over her head. She was damned stunning at what she did.

"Thanks. Are you busy tonight?" she asked.

"Not as long as the show goes as planned. You gonna call and talk dirty to me?" She was in New York and he was in Sacramento. There was no way they could actually get together.

"I have cannoli. You can order carrot cake from room service. We can have dessert together."

Troy poked his head around the curtain, looking damned dire. "Sounds good, darlin'. I'll text you when you I'm on the way to the hotel."

"Sounds excellent. I— Later, Ace."

"Yeah." For a moment he'd been sure she was going to say it, but she hadn't. *Damn it.* "I miss you."

"You, too." She hung up, and Ace glared at Troy. "What now?"

"We need to get ahold of Lorenzo Morales, see if he has a horse Adam can use for tonight."

"You're kidding." Adam Taggart was their safety man, who worked the arena on horseback. "What happened to Baby Blue?" he asked, meaning Adam's best gelding.

"Kicked the rail and cut the shit out of his leg."

"Fuck a duck." Ace rubbed the back of his neck, not liking how this night was shaping up. They'd be damned lucky if no one fucking died. "I'll call Lorenzo.

You see who we can scare up to replace Nate. Coke is still only at half speed and Coop needs to retire."

"You got it." Troy ducked out, and Ace didn't even have a moment to say a prayer for a safe night before three other people were vying for his attention.

Man, it was gonna be a long evening.

* * * *

"Mexico City was a bust," Kitty said, resisting the urge to shuffle the papers in front of her. Her notes were precise, concise and chock-full of suggestions about where she could follow the cartel story next. She only hoped she had a chance to make her spiel. Tom Frendy, the producer sitting across the table at their martini lunch, seemed…bored.

"I know. I think we've played out all the goodwill we can with you being a blonde."

"Oh?" She did straighten the edges of the papers now. "So, where am I going next?"

"Some studio work here in town. I want you to work on that Dubai footage with a new producer we hired. He's young, has a fresh perspective. Have you thought about the procedures I suggested?"

Her mouth tightened and she tried hard not to simply unload on him. He'd sent her an email.

Get work on the eyes, get lip injections, see surgeon about implants.

She had it printed out to go to HR in case he tried to fire her ass when she said no.

"I read it. I haven't made any determinations yet."

"Well, it's not like I think you're ugly, Kitty." He sighed, leaning across the table. "Have you seen your competition lately? Tia Martinez. Lush, 34D, sultry and comfortingly ethnic. The day of the blonde and the Asian is done. People want more exotic."

"Wow." She took one sheet of paper off the top of the pile and handed it over. "Here are some suggestions about Mexico. I sent a copy to Al, just in case he needed it." Al was this one's boss, and still liked her, so her ideas wouldn't go to someone more exotic. "I'll work on the Dubai footage, but I want first call if we move on the cartel story."

Now his face was the one tightening into a mask. "Of course. No problem."

"Good. Thanks for lunch." She tossed back her drink and stood. Damn it, Ace's friends kept telling her she was a star. Maybe it was time she began acting like one.

Chapter Fourteen

Kitty walked out of the doctor's office, feeling a little like she'd been kicked.

Pregnant.

She... There was no way.

Her? Pregnant?

With Ace Porter's baby?

She hurried along the street, head down, ignoring the crowds. She was supposed to fly to Juarez tomorrow. Then head south with Leroy to see if they could get Tia Martinez out from Miguel Nueces' hands.

She couldn't be pregnant.

She looked at the paper in her hand, those numbers undeniable.

Pregnant.

God.

She paused in front of a coffee shop, then kept moving. No. Chocolate maybe, but not coffee. She thought about calling Ace, but decided on Honey instead.

Honey's voice sounded happy and warm. "Hey, Kitty-Kat! How's it going?"

She opened her mouth to speak but instead burst into tears.

"Kitty? What? Where are you? Do I need to send Leroy to get you?"

"I...Honey... I..." She stepped into an alleyway, checking to make sure she was alone. "I'm pregnant."

"Pregnant!" Honey's voice rose to something like a shout. "Well, sweetie! My goodness."

"I'm... Oh, God. Honey. What do I do?" She couldn't get swollen on camera, or call Ace and say 'hey, I trapped you'! She couldn't do this.

"Oh, honey, women have been having babies for ages."

"Sure, but I'm here, in New York. With Ace's baby."

"You should call him." Honey was always so calm and steady.

"And tell him what? Oh, by the way, I'm heading to Juarez tomorrow, I'm blonde, worth money and pregnant?" She was feeling a little hysterical.

"Kitty! You can't go to Juarez."

"I have to. You know that." Tia was there. The girl was a frigging features reporter and some stupid executive had sent her down instead of Kitty for the cartel story and she'd disappeared.

"No, I don't. I think you're being silly. Ace is crazy about you."

"The plane leaves in eighteen hours, Honey."

"I know." Honey sounded glum. "I know you have to go find that girl. Leroy said. But you need to tell Ace."

"I...I don't know. I didn't do this on purpose, I swear. I was on the pill." She felt a little like a teenager confessing to her mom, which was just stupid.

"Oh, sweetie. Believe me when I tell you that you can be on the pill and he can be snipped and it can still happen."

She stopped, then laughed, hard. "You're so right. God, I'm going to have to tell him or break up with him."

On her frame, she only had a couple of months before there was a baby bump. He would know. He watched her show now.

"Tell him." Now Honey had her mommy voice on.

"I... I'll call him. See if he's busy."

"There you go. You can do this, Kitty."

"I guess." She sighed softly. "It's due in March."

"Well, when you get back we'll have a shower."

"Maybe. I've got to get through Mexico, then the fall, winter, telling Ace, getting fat..."

"Katherine Carpenter you stop that. This is going to be wonderful. You'll see."

"What if I suck at it? Being a mom? What if Ace hates me?"

"Ace doesn't hate you. Why would you say that?" Honey chastised.

"He doesn't want some woman trying to trap him into marriage." Not that she was doing that. She'd say yes, if he asked. Well, if he asked for some reason other than the baby.

"Huh. I'm sending Leroy tomorrow."

"No, Honey. I'm meeting Leroy there tomorrow, remember?" Here to Houston to El Paso, then to the border by car.

"Oh. Okay. Well, come tonight."

"I'll see if I can. I have to pack."

"I want to see you. I'll call the agency." Honey knew how to make shit happen, and she'd made emergency travel plans more than once for her and Leroy.

"I love you." Honey was the closest thing she'd had to a mom in a long time.

"I love you, too, Kitty. You just breathe."

"Breathe. Right." Her phone beeped and she looked. Ace. *Oh. Oh, God.* "It's him. Calling."

"So talk to him. I'll see you before you leave."

"Okay. Okay." She clicked over, still breathing a little hard. "Hey, you."

"Hey, darlin'." She could hear his smile in his voice and it made her breath flood her chest.

She headed toward home. "How're you today? Busy?"

"Yeah. Running like a mad fool. Got some time tomorrow, though, thought I'd see if we have a layover anywhere near."

"I'm in the air most of the day tomorrow. Where are you going to be?" Maybe that way she could tell him to his face.

"Saint Louis." She could hear him mumble a little, maybe to one of the guys.

"I'll be in Atlanta on my layover, sorry. I'm sorry I'm going to miss you." She couldn't tell him if he was with other people. That wasn't fair.

"Oh. I— Where are you headed?"

"Juarez, then into the interior." They'd talked about this. For a second.

"You're going to Mexico again?" His voice rose with what sounded like alarm.

"I have to. There's a journalist there that needs some help."

"If they need to extract someone they can hire some burly man, darlin'."

"That would be Leroy." She chuckled softly. "They've asked for me, specifically. They're offering an exclusive. It's a huge break in the story."

"It's crazy is what it is. You barely got out the last time, darlin'."

"Hey, Mexico City was last time, and it was a breeze."

"Well, now, that wasn't Juarez, was it? This gal you're going after is missing, isn't she?" Now he was getting mad. She'd never heard it directed at her, really, but she'd heard it when someone in his league screwed up.

"I have to go. It's important." Tia was there, and this might be her chance to make a desk job, which she would totally need if she was having a baby."

"When are you coming back, then? I think we need to talk." Ace snarled something that she couldn't hear, obviously trying to get a few more moments to talk to her.

"I'm supposed to be back in two weeks, depending on how far into the interior we end up." There was no way she was going to drop the bomb about the baby now. No way.

"Okay." He mumbled something else, then sighed. "Be careful, darlin'. Please? I'll see you when you get home. I really want to talk over some shit. Okay?"

"I'm always careful. I...I really miss you." *More than ever.*

"God, I miss you, too, Kitty. You have any trouble, you call me, you got it? I can be there in hours, and Lucky's right down there..."

"I will. I...we do have to talk, though. Okay? After?"

"Yeah. Yeah, okay. I— Shit. I got to go. I'll clear a couple weeks when you get back. We'll go to the Bahamas or something."

"Okay. Somewhere quiet. Bye, Ace."

"Bye, darlin'." The line went dead.

So much for telling him.

It was probably for the best, really. She was busy, he was busy. Hell, women lost babies all the time, and she didn't have time to think about it, at least not right now. Guilt speared through her, because she was telling herself hideous lies, but her job had been her life for too long.

Right now she had a story to chase.

Chapter Fifteen

"No, the arena is too damned small." Ace sighed, rolling his head on his neck. They were heading into the finals, doing the last three or four big events, and they had a new damned arena to deal with in Topeka. It was smaller, because the arena they usually played was under construction to fix a massive leak.

Adam Taggart was pitching a bitch about having no room for his horse in there, and Ace couldn't blame him. So they were trying to make space.

He grinned at Troy, his stock manager. "Can't you move the chutes back three feet?"

"Sure, fuckhead. Let me make it November while I'm at it, and make it to where the Brazilians aren't eight out of the top ten so the sponsors stop bitching."

Ace flipped Troy off because it was required of him, and let Angie stick a clipboard in his face to sign a bunch of papers. Shit, wasn't Sandy the CEO or whatever so someone else signed stuff? "Well, Adam can't ride a Shetland, buddy."

"No? You sure? I could get one in here in a New York minute. I keep telling the clown he needs more animals in his act. You 'member that guy with the de-scented skunk?"

Ace held up a hand. "Don't even. Dillon bitched for six months when he had to go watch that guy."

Troy chuckled, mustache bouncing with each puff of air. "Man, these newfangled cowboys…"

"Yeah. Pussies." His phone rang in his pocket and Ace felt a moment of hope that it would be Kitty. He hadn't heard from her in three weeks, and he was plumb worried.

It wasn't her, though.

Hell, it was some number he didn't even know, so he ignored it.

Through three more rings, even.

Then it came again.

Shit. He waved Troy off for a minute and went to the corner of the battle room before answering. "Hello?"

"Ace? Ace, is that you?" It was a woman, and she was *upset*.

"Yes, ma'am." The voice niggled at him, but he just couldn't place it.

"It's Honey. Leroy's wife."

"Well, hey, Honey. What's wrong?" He knew something had to be bad for her to be calling him. He hoped bad wasn't *bad*.

"Leroy sent me a card. In the mail." She took a hitching breath. "I called the station and talked to them, but they aren't listening and with Kitty being there…"

"Okay, now." He headed outside, needing to be sure he wouldn't drop the call or get interrupted. "Start from the beginning, Honey."

"They headed into the interior, to try and get that little entertainment girl, but Leroy's phone cut off two weeks ago. I got a card yesterday and it said 'don't raise the red flag'. That's our signal for 'we're in big trouble'."

"Shit." Ace's mind started racing. He could get to Mexico in just a few hours, but he needed a place to start. "Does the card have a postmark?"

"Four days ago. I wouldn't have called, but with Kitty's condition and all, I'm scared for her."

"Her condition." That distracted him for a minute as easily as if someone had popped him on the nose.

"Yeah. The baby. I just…we have to get them home."

The baby. His mouth fell open, and for a moment he couldn't talk. If Honey meant Kitty was pregnant he was gonna… Well, get her back safe, then kill her.

"Ace? Are you there?"

"I am. I need you to get everything together that you have, Honey. Names and dates and the postcard and everything. I'll be on the next flight to Houston, okay? I have to make a bunch of calls."

"Just tell me when to pick you up. Thank you. I'm just…they won't listen. Leroy never used the code word — not even in Baghdad."

Baghdad.

Jesus.

"I'll call with my flight number and all. Don't you worry, Honey. We'll get them out right and tight."

"Okay. Okay. Thank you." The phone went dead.

He shut his phone and stared at it. Baby. A baby. Shit. He sprinted inside, his boots ringing on the concrete. "Angie!"

The production assistant looked up, eyes wide. "Ace? What's wrong? Who's hurt?"

"I need a flight to Houston." His ready bag was still in his rental because he'd checked out of the hotel that morning. Today was short go day. "Call me when you have something. I'm on my way to the airport."

"Houston. Got it, Boss. I'll call you." She was a good girl. Solid as a rock.

He nodded and headed out, Troy right there on his heel. "Your momma okay?"

"Yeah. Shit, can you call her? Tell her I'll be out of the country for a few days?"

"I can. Don't worry—I got your back here. We're solid."

"Thanks, man. I need to get ahold of Lucky, too. Cash always has a better time with that. Can you tell him to tell Lucky I need him to be near a phone?"

His bag was right there, and he wavered. Cab or rental? He could get someone else to turn in the truck, even if he parked it at the airport.

"I'll turn your truck in. Just go. You want me to get Steele?"

"I'll call him from the road." He would get Steele to take on Sandy and keep shit going. "Thanks, man. I'll holler at y'all as soon as I know when I'll be back."

"'Kay. Be safe."

There was nothing like a friend who knew when not to ask questions.

Troy was sort of like a young uncle to him and the other Horsemen, always had been. Ace hit the highway and headed toward the airport, his head hurting a little with all the shit going through it. They'd started in Juarez and gone in, so Lucky wasn't going to be much help where he was on the coast. Still, there was no telling where they were. Shit, four weeks? They could be anywhere.

Baby.

It hit him again, how she'd sounded so alone the last time, how she'd wanted to talk to him.

Fuck. He should have made the time instead of brushing her off because he was pissed about Mexico.

Ace tightened his grip on the steering wheel, knowing he had to concentrate on now.

If Leroy was scared enough to worry Honey, it was a big fucking deal. He'd seen how that man looked at his wife.

Christ. He almost hit someone when he changed lanes, hitting the split in the highway.

Angie called before he parked the truck. "I have you on a flight leaving in three hours, non-stop to Houston on United."

"Thanks, lady." He'd see if he could get standby on something earlier, but Angie was almost inhumanly organized. "I'll be leaving the truck in short-term. I'll call Troy and let him know a row and space."

"Good deal. You need anything else, Boss?"

"Not right now. Just keep the show going, huh?" He knew she could do it on her own if she had to.

"You know it. Emmy and I are on it."

"I owe you a bonus." He hung up, pulling the truck into the short-term garage. He grabbed his bag, his hat and his laptop case. Thankfully, he always had his passport with him when he traveled. Mexico would let him in.

He got his ticket, got through security, then found the gate and grabbed his laptop and Googled Mexico.

About four pages in, he heard someone clear his throat.

Ace glanced up, ready to snarl because he wasn't in anyone's way. Which was when he started trying not to smile, instead. Two cowboys stood there, one lean and brown, with shrewd brown eyes under the brim of a summer straw Stetson, and one barrel-chested and stocky, all blue eyes and five-o'clock shadow.

Steele Flannagan and Cash McClellan, two of his best friends on earth. "How in hell did y'all get through security?"

Steele grinned, only one side of his mouth quirking. "Ang got us tickets. First class, huh? Fancy. What's in Houston?"

They sat, one on either side of him.

"My girlfriend's cameraman's wife." That was really the easiest thing to do with the members of the group the media used to call the Four Horsemen. Tell the truth.

"Your girlfriend's..." Cash started.

"Cameraman's wife," Steele finished. "Wow."

"Yeah." He sighed. "Said girlfriend is in Mexico with the cameraman, and they're in trouble."

Steele nodded. "Well, she must be something, to head out in the middle of a show. So here we are, man."

"I got a thing in with Lucky's cantina friends. We'll call right before we board. This girl the one that met him already?" Cash asked Steele.

"Yeah. Her name's Kitty." God, had he not introduced her to Steele and Cash?

Steele grinned, a little wolfishly. "She's a TV reporter. Tiny little thing. Funny...I always thought Ace was queer."

Ace stopped his fist inches from Steele's nose, knowing airport security would have his ass if he connected. "Shut up."

"Nah. He's only a teeny little critter that needs a wee woman." Cash chuckled. Asshole had always been too big to be a decent rider.

Ace snorted. "Teeny and in Mexico she's still more'n y'all have." He frowned. "Last time she was down there she was almost kidnapped by a drug lord, you know? Second to last time."

Cash's eyes went wide and Steele's eyebrows lowered dangerously. "Kidnapped? Ace? You'd best start talking now. She in trouble?"

"Honey says so, yeah. She got a message from Leroy, that's Kitty's cameraman, and she says it's their prearranged signal. Network won't do squat." He felt better already with his friends there to help.

"Well, then. I guess we'll mount up." Steele looked about as sure as anything.

"Yessir. We need to meet her."

"Thanks, y'all." Ace rubbed his face with one hand. "I was so mad at her for going to Mexico. It wasn't real pretty, last time we talked."

"Eh. It'll make for great sex after you fetch her." Steele was a horndog.

"Yeah, but first we got to get her. How long from Houston to where they're holding her?" Cash was way more practical.

"Shit, man, I don't know. Honey got a card in the mail from four days ago. We'll have to start there."

"Damn." Cash shook his head. "Okay, I've got a couple calls to make. I'll be over there." Cash waved vaguely toward a fairly quiet corner, heading off to pull out his phone.

Ace grinned at Steele a little. "This sucks, man."

"No shit. We'll get her back to you." No doubt, there. None. The man was solid.

"Yeah. I just—" He glanced around to make sure no one was paying any mind. "She's pregnant, Steele."

He'd never seen Steele look that shocked, not even when Beau Lafitte beat Marcos Sanchez down so bad the man needed ten thousand dollars' worth of dental work after. "No shit?"

"Yeah." He spread his hands. "I just found out."

"Oh. I was wondering why you let her go off." Steele took a deep breath. "Guess that's why y'all needed to have that talk, huh?"

"That would be it." He shook his head. Damn it all. "This waiting is getting to me."

"We could go drink and pick a fight. I got cards in my bag."

Cash came over, eyes wide. "Lucky says your woman sent him a little beat-up girl. Says she got traded out."

His hands clenched. "What?"

Cash shrugged. "Says this little gal shows up this morning, all bruised and scared, with a message that Ace's girl told her to find him, that he'd find you, get help. Says this dude's had her damn near a month and your girl—Kathy is it?—was the trade."

Steele just groaned.

Ace shot to his feet, not sure what the hell he was gonna do, but unable to sit a minute longer. "I got to— Shit, I can drive there faster than I can do all this waiting."

"Bullshit we can." Cash looked at him like he was crazy. "Shit, man. Lucky's got someone who knows exactly where the fuck she is. How is this bad? We get to Houston, we charter a plane, we get the Luckster, we go fetch her. We're at the beach by noon tomorrow."

Steele gave Cash an incredulous look. "Dude, she's knocked up."

Cash dropped his phone on the floor. "Well, fuckadoodle. Why the hell'd you let her go to fucking Mexico, Ace?"

"I didn't know!" He was going to hit something.

"That Mexico was scary?"

Steele snorted. "No, dipshit. He didn't know she was preggers."

"Man, that's a little important, don't you think?" Now Cash looked at him like he was stupid.

"Yes." Ace gritted his teeth, spitting the words out between them. "I was an ass. She didn't tell me. Can we get to the plan?"

"First, Cash picks his phone up." Steele was so fucking helpful.

"I need a beer, too."

"This is not helping." He snapped his laptop closed and stuffed it away, intent on finding a flight that left now, not an hour from now.

"Where're we going?" Cash touched his arm. "Look. This is fucking Topeka, asshole. Not DFW. Let's charter our flight and we need to wire Lucky some cash." At their stares Cash shrugged. "I ain't going to fight a fucking drug lord without ammunition, y'all. Them boys got guns and Lucky knows how to load us up. Plus we'll need transportation."

Ace took a deep breath. "Right. Okay. Right." Cash was absolutely correct. That was something to do, at least. "You get Lucky the money. Steele, don't you know someone who does shit out of Houston?"

"Yes, sir. I'll have a plane waiting on us. You need to talk to that lady from Houston that called you?"

"I'll call Honey." Ace took one breath, then another. He could do this. No one could get shit done like his cowboys. Especially when they had a plan.

He could only hope they weren't too late.

Chapter Sixteen

If she threw up one more time, she was going to lose it.

Kitty wiped her mouth, rinsed it out. She supposed she should be grateful they had her in a room with a bathroom.

Today should be another 'interview' day, if Marco held to his normal schedule. Those days were hard. They ended with him raving for hours, and twice he'd had women assassinated right in front of her. Once he'd pulled a gun and shot the chair where she was sitting, so close that she had a deep scratch on her upper arm.

She'd convinced him to let Tia go, though, and she'd told her to go to Lucky. Ace would come.

Kitty didn't know why she believed it, but she did.

She put her hand over her belly, which was starting to be the littlest bit round. "You hold on, now. You have to hold on for me."

A tap at the window made her squeal, jump. Leroy. *Oh, God.*

She hurried over, looked through the bars. "Why are you outside?"

"I demanded exercise. They're a little afraid I'm going to go all bulgy and green, I think." He leaned close enough that she could see the lines around his mouth, his bloodshot eyes. "How you doin', baby girl?"

"Okay. Little scared. I got Tia out. Sent her to Lucky."

That meant that they only had to worry about them. It also meant that she was the one in line for Marco's rage.

"She gonna make it?" Leroy'd had kind of had a rage episode when they'd first arrived, when he'd seen poor Tia and her garden of bruises.

"She is." She had to. Please, God. The girl was surprisingly tough for a human interest chickie.

"Rock on." Leroy touched the window. "I made them let me send Honey a note. She'll know now, baby girl. She'll get help."

She closed her eyes a second. "I think he'll let you go, too. You know what he wants."

And it wasn't a huge rumbly Texan like Leroy.

"Nope. I'm sticking with you like glue, Kitty." He had his serious face pasted on, a growl in his deep voice.

"Promise?" Her hand touched his on the glass.

"I promise, baby. I got your back, remember? Baghdad to Zacatecas."

She nodded. "That's right. He wants to film today. That means we get tomorrow to rest."

"Okay. We'll get our breath and plan for when the cavalry comes." He grinned, looking just like him on any day for a moment. "And if they don't come, we'll make a plan for taking ourselves right out of here."

"You know it." She winked. "My pants aren't going to fit much longer, no matter how bad the food is, huh?"

"Yeah." His smile disappeared. "You'll have to start wearing my shirts."

That cracked her up, her laughter ringing out, and it felt right. No, amazing.

"I love you, Big Daddy. I swear. You're my best friend. I'm going to get you home to Honey. I will."

"I know. I love you, baby." He sighed. "I need to move on, or they'll come poke my kidneys with a stick." He winked. "Be strong."

"You too."

She didn't stay to watch him walk away.

Ace would come.

He would.

He had to.

Kitty needed him.

* * * *

Lucky met them at a tiny airfield situated where Chihuahua started to give way to Sonora. The Juarez cartel held sway here, according to what Ace had read, and man, Juarez wasn't pretty these days. Neither was the Chihuahua desert. Oh, at any other time he would have found the rugged landscape pretty. Not now. Not when he got a load of the pretty little gal next to Lucky. The bruised and battered little gal.

Ace gave Lucky a man hug. "Hey, man."

"Ace." Lucky looked well and truly pissed off. "This here's Tia. Your girl sent her over to me for safekeeping."

"Howdy, Tia." He shook her itty bitty hand, studying her black and blue face. He was gonna kill something. If they'd laid a hand on Kitty, he'd kill lots of somethings.

"Mr. Porter." She offered him a shaky smile. "Kitty said you'd come."

"Did she now? Sorry to take you away from the beach." He smiled back, gentle as he could be at the moment. "Kitty said you were the bravest girl she knew."

She snorted. "She made them let me go. He... Marco's killing people, shooting them, and she didn't even flinch. She just stares him down. She's my hero." Tia puffed up, clearly ready to go fight to get Kitty back.

Ace just... He was gonna lose it. He swallowed the lump in his throat. "Mine, too. So, what have we got?"

Lucky shrugged. "We got a Hummer coming. I got munitions. I got a basic idea where they got her. Tia here says they let Leroy out to exercise once a day and that they shoot camera interviews every other day." Lucky's voice dropped. "Those get rough. The guy is an egomaniac who likes to rant and rave to an audience."

Ace grunted and Steele and Cash finally joined them after gathering their shit and talking to the pilot about being ready to get them out of Dodge.

"Let's go back to my place—pack the vehicle, get ready."

"Wait. Isn't that out of our way, man?" He didn't mean to be all grr, but that seemed like a waste of time.

"It's out of the way, but it's mine and the *Federales* aren't hunting me." Lucky stared him down. "I'm waiting to hear from a guy whose wife's sister cooks over at the compound where Kitty is being held."

"Okay." Ace sighed and rolled his head on his neck. "Yeah."

His Kitty was out there with a crazy son of a bitch with guns.

His girl.

Steele clapped him on one shoulder. "We'll get her, brother. I swear to you. If I have to shoot every bastard between here and the border."

Ace managed a grin for his best friend. "I know. I just worry, is all. How was she when you left, Miss Tia?"

"Okay. Sick, I think. She threw up a lot. Marco shot her chair once, scratched her arm pretty bad. But he hadn't had them…" She shrugged, winced, motioned to her poor face. "You know."

Lucky growled and puffed up and Ace nodded. What sort of asshole did you have to be to beat on a little gal like this?

"Let's get moving, y'all. It don't feel right, just standing out here like targets." Cash got them going, face like a thundercloud. Cash didn't have a girl of his own, really, but the man had sisters — four of 'em — and he had opinions on how a woman ought to be treated.

They got their bags and all into the truck Lucky had driven in, and Ace and Cash and Steele started mapping the route from Lucky's to the spot Tia had pinpointed on the map. A white ball of rage crouched in the pit of his belly, burning through him like fire.

Ace knew he had to use that, not let it stop him in his tracks. Good thing he'd learned a few things about channeling his energy over the years of being an athlete.

"We got to get a message in for her, if we can." Cash frowned. "Or the guy. Can he help us? He a solid man?"

"He's the best." Ace knew Leroy was solid as a rock. "He'll be waiting for someone to make a move. He'll make one himself, we don't hurry."

"Fuckin' A." Steele nodded. "I like to hear that. We get Lucky's housecleaner girl to warn him, maybe get him a gun. That little gal said they let him exercise."

"That way we have someone on the inside. That works."

"One of us has to stay outside, to drive." Cash looked at him. "Cain't be you, Ace. She'll go with you."

"Lucky," Steele said immediately. "It's not his land, I know, but he's the closest thing we have to a citizen."

Cash snorted, raising his voice. "That and he's so little."

Right on cue, that middle finger came up, flipping them off.

Ace grinned. "He's gonna be the best long distance cover we have, too. You got a long-range gun, Luck?"

"I got your back, man. I ain't letting this go bad."

"I know." He wanted to thank all of them, just for being there, but they'd give him shit for being a sap.

Cash looked over at Lucky, at the wee lady next to him, shook his head, started rumbling some.

Ace ducked his head a little and Steele chuckled. "Cash will tear the man apart with his bare hands, buddy."

He met Steele's eyes. "Only if I get there second."

Chapter Seventeen

A hard hand grabbed her by the hair, dragged her up. "*Vamanos, puta.*"

"Stop. What the hell? Where's Marco?" Kitty stumbled along, hands grabbing the goon's wrists.

Oh, God.

Not yet.

The man twisted his hand to get a better grip, pulling her out of her room and down the hall she'd been down so many times. They were going toward the interview room.

"No!"

The last one had been bad, Marco raving and throwing things. She'd ended with a highball glass glancing off her cheek, and when she'd come to, Leroy had been fighting a couple of assholes, one eye swelled shut and the bastard's boot on her throat.

She couldn't do it again already.

Gunfire went off somewhere out in the compound, startling her guard so much he almost dropped her. She knew that sound. This wasn't Marco shooting chickens. This was semi-automatic spray.

"Ace." *Please, God. Please.*

She let herself go limp, and when he let go, Kitty made herself run hard, searching furiously for a door.

She heard shouts, heard the guard scrambling, but she was focused on freedom. Which was why she screamed with frustration when the door she opened revealed Marco behind it.

He grabbed her throat. "You bitch! What did you do?"

Kitty clawed at his hands, knowing if she let him keep touching her he would kill her. Kill her baby. Ace's baby. She kicked out as hard as she could, connecting with Marco's balls.

He wheezed, his face turning almost purple, and went to his knees. She ducked the clawed hand of the guard who'd caught up with her and ran.

"Ace! Ace!" She screamed, the sound harsh and weird, slamming into someone as she hurtled down the hallway. "No!"

"Kitty." Hard hands closed on her shoulder, but they weren't hurtful. "Get behind me, darlin'."

"Ace. It's you. Leroy's here." She stared at him. "You came."

"I did. Leroy's with Cash." He started easing her down the hall, one hand holding her.

"He's back here." She coughed a little, her throat swelling some. "Marco."

"I need to get you to Steele." Ace sounded grimly determined. "He's just at the end of the hall."

A bang sounded, the wall beside her almost disappearing. "Ace! Run!"

Ace grabbed her up almost in a football hold and ran.

They ran into another cowboy, who was holding a rifle and frowning. "You got her?"

"I do. I need you to get her to Lucky." Ace handed her off and headed back toward Marco.

"Ace!" She struggled, pulling at Steele's arms. "Please, Ace!"

"What, darlin'?" Ace stopped to stare at her. "He's never coming near you again."

"He'll hurt you. He'll—" Another shot came, then another, and the sound echoed violently, her knees going weak, the dark hall going black.

* * * *

Ace sprinted the last few feet to the Hummer, putting Kitty gently in one of the seats before counting heads. Steele, Cash, Lucky, Leroy, Tia, who'd insisted on coming to help Lucky…

"Go, buddy! Go, go, go." He hopped in, ready to hang on.

"Going." Lucky slammed it into gear, the Hummer's tires squealing.

"She okay? Tell me she's okay? Baby girl…" Leroy looked fucking gray.

Ace nodded. "She's all right, man. She passed out, but she's all right." Ace had to believe that. Even though she hadn't made a peep.

"That motherfucker…" The huge man was vibrating, shaking but good.

"You okay, Leroy? Not bleeding?" If anyone needed triage, they'd have to wait until it was safe to stop.

"I ain't bleeding." Those dark eyes met his. "I want to get home and see my woman. She call you?"

"She did. She got your card. They sent it from El Paso, though, so we had a tough time finding you."

"Good girl." Leroy leaned his head back.

"We'll call her when we get somewhere safe, man." He glanced at Steele, who nodded and got out water bottles and power bars to pass around.

He turned his attention to his Kitty. Her throat was black and blue and there was a vicious swelling on one side of her face. She looked drawn, and damn it, he wanted her to wake up for him. *Now.*

He pulled his bandana out of his pocket and got it wet, dabbing at her face.

Her eyes opened suddenly. "Ace. Ace, he's going to hurt you."

"Shh. No, darlin'. I'm right here. We're safe." *Mostly.*

"Ace..." She stared at him. "You came. I knew you would."

Her voice sounded like she was a smoker.

"I did. I'm sorry I didn't come sooner." He kissed her mouth gently, needing to feel her.

Her fingers touched his cheek, shaking some.

It was like they were alone suddenly, instead of in a bumpy Hummer with his best friends and two of her colleagues. Well, Leroy was family.

Her eyes closed and she leaned against him, quiet. Hiding.

He stroked her hair, wanting to go back and pump more bullets into that Marco guy, even if they wouldn't be self-defense this time. That greasy motherfucker wasn't ever hurting another woman again.

Ever.

He kissed her temple, his heart finally starting to slow down.

"What's the plan, man? Where we goin'?" Leroy sounded like he'd aged twenty years.

"We're going to Lucky's, Leroy. We'll go from there to Houston." They'd all rest a few hours.

"Okay. Soon. I want back in Texas."

"I know. I know." He did. No one could touch them at the ranch. They had to regroup, though.

"I want a beer. Possibly a steak." Steele looked at Kitty. "You need to feed her more."

"I feed her just fine," Ace snapped. "I can't be responsible for murdering drug lords."

"No? Well, shit, brother. What good are you, then?"

He stared at Steele, his lips twitching.

Asshole.

Steele grinned at him, nodded once, then leaned back and closed his eyes.

Damn. Cash was taping up something on Leroy's arm, Lucky drove, and that little Tia girl stared straight ahead, lips pressed together. All in all, he thought it had gone well.

Now he needed to get his girl home.

Chapter Eighteen

Kitty sat at the edge of the water and watched the sun come up.

She knew she'd slept, knew somebody'd put bandages on her cheek, her arm, and there were fresh, soft clothes on her. Ace had been sound asleep when she'd woken, hit the bathroom and gone to sit and cry a little, give thanks.

She heard the sand crunch and she looked up, expecting Ace.

It was Tia instead.

"Hey, you. You did it." She reached up, squeezed Tia's hand. "Thank you." Tia was a brave woman, and Kitty owed her big for trusting her.

Tia offered her a watery smile. "You're hurt. Did he…? Are you…?"

"Just bruises. I promise." Her throat was the worst of it.

"I'm glad to hear it." Tia sat next to her, folding into a very small space. "Thank you. For getting me out."

She nodded. "Where are you going now? I can talk to my people, if you want."

"I don't know." Tia shrugged. "I'm not sure I'm cut out for serious news, and the network will be kissing my ass. I may stay at the beach for a bit."

"It's beautiful here." She wanted to go home.

"Lucky says I can stay a few days, huh?" Tia smiled, and this time it was stronger. "When do you leave?"

"I don't remember. Soon. Leroy needs to see Honey." She was sure someone had said, but...it was all a little distant.

"Of course. Your Ace, he was—"

"He's my hero." She'd known he would come for her, like she knew the sun rose in the morning. Ace would always come for her.

"He and his cowboys are a force of nature."

Kitty teared up, but she smiled. "They are."

"They'll be waiting for you. The vultures. Don't let them see you cry."

"Never." She winked. "I'm a pro."

"I know. You're *my* hero, Kitty."

She patted Tia's hand, a lump in her throat. God, she wanted to go home to the ranch.

Tia squeezed her hand. "Thank you again." Then Tia knelt up and gave her a quick, impulsive hug. "Good luck, *amiga.*"

Tia left her sitting there, tears in her eyes, which was how Ace found her a few minutes later.

"You okay, darlin'?" He put a hand on her shoulder, peering down at her.

"Yeah. Yeah, I will be. You?" His touch was warm, solid.

"I'm better now that I got you safe." He sat next to her, his thin sleep pants soaked through by the damp sand.

"I knew you'd come. I knew it." She'd never once doubted him. He was her cowboy.

"As soon as I knew you needed me, darlin'." His fingers caught hers. He was staring out at the ocean, his jaw tight. "I'm sorry I snarled at you, last time we talked."

"You were busy. I… We have to talk, though. Really." She had to tell him. Hell, she was showing a little already, because she'd lost weight.

"We do." He glanced over, hazel eyes bright in the early morning light.

Okay, Katherine. Do this before you leave. If he freaks, you go to Honey's.

"I…I have to tell you that… I…" She sighed, put on her reporter face, one hand protectively on her belly. "I'm pregnant, Ace. I'm sorry. I didn't try to trap you or anything, I just…"

She was keeping the baby.

Ace stared at her, lips twitching. "Don't be any dumber than you have to be, darlin'. All you had to do was say."

She searched his eyes, then took one of Ace's hands, placed it on her belly. "March. It's due in March."

"March, huh?" *Oh. Oh, look at that smile.* She'd been so scared.

"Yes." She touched his lips with trembling fingers. "I want to go home, Ace."

"Me, too. We're gonna have some talks then, too." He nodded, climbing to his feet and holding a hand down for her.

She took it, let him help her up and wrap one arm around her.

They wandered back toward Lucky's place, feet in the sand, the smell of bacon strong in the air.

Leroy looked up then rushed her, scooping her up. "Baby Girl. I swear to God, if I never see some asshole with his foot on your throat again…"

"Leroy…" That was going to make Ace bitchy.

"It's true." Leroy looked hard at Ace. "What took you so long?"

Ace stared back. "We got there, didn't we?"

"Eventually." Leroy kept hold of her. "Are you going to take care of her now?"

"Leroy!" Now that was ridiculous.

Ace nodded sharply. "I am. We're flying into Houston today. We'll see Honey, then go to the ranch."

"Excellent plan. She needs to see a doctor and she needs you." Leroy put her down, got right in Ace's face. "You're ever evil to her, or to that baby, and I will beat your ass down. Got it?"

Ace didn't puff up or get angry. He met Leroy's eyes and held out one rough, square hand. "You got my word that you'll never have to."

Leroy shook Ace's hand, then pulled the man in for a rough hug while they all stared. "Good. You'll be an acceptable daddy to our little peanut."

"Peanut." Ace hooted. "I like it. You ready to have breakfast and hit the road?"

Steele laughed loud, coming in from the back, toweling his hair. "I am, man. Outdoor showers suck."

Kitty grinned. "I don't know. Lucky's showers aren't too bad."

The big cowboy looked over, snorted. "Yeah, if you're a midget like Ace and Lucky."

Lucky hooted. "You're unnaturally large, Cash-man. Deal."

Leroy flexed. "He ain't that big."

Cash headed over, grabbed Lucky by the head and gave the man a noogie. "Lucky's just a baby."

Lucky sputtered, wiggling, and Steele grinned up at Leroy. "We'll have to call you Gigantor."

"I like it."

Leroy grinned and Kitty cracked up, laughing hard enough it made her a little dizzy.

Ace put an arm around her, leading her to a chair and lowering her down. "Lucky made some juice."

"Sounds good." She closed her eyes a second, face to the sun.

It was going to be okay.

It had to be.

Ace was there. The rest was just details.

Chapter Nineteen

They got to Houston mid-afternoon, which sucked, because traffic would be a bear. Ace hoped to God Honey was waiting for them, and that she'd thought to keep a low profile.

They stepped out of security, the flashbulbs and the screaming mass of press making his heart sink a little. Leroy and Cash stepped in front of them, Steele sliding next to Kitty, just like clockwork. Kitty's hand dug into his arm.

Ace patted her hand before putting his other arm around her and ducking them down. No one could get to her.

"Katherine! Katherine, can you tell us how you escaped? Is it true Marco Nueces was assassinated? Were you injured?"

The questions came blaring out and Kitty pressed closer to him.

They headed toward the door, leaving the crush of people behind. There was another, bigger set of vultures waiting for them on the other side of that.

Honey was there, though, along with a bunch of suits who headed straight for Kitty.

Ace held his ground, knowing they had to get through all this shit. He wasn't going to let them be separated, though.

He put his passport away first, then waited for his girl. Honey was in Leroy's arms already, holding on tight. When Kitty came through, she went straight to him, eyes panicked. "Ace. Take me home."

"I got you, darlin'." He took her in his arms, hugging her close for a moment, waiting for the Horsemen to fall in and help make way.

"Katherine Carpenter. We need to talk."

Steele turned and looked at them. "Y'all Feds?"

"Pardon me?"

"I want to see badges."

"We're from the network in New York. Her employers."

Steele snorted, stood there like a wall. "You ain't cops? That little girl ain't got to talk to nobody 'less her husband says she has to or you got a badge that has Texas written on it."

Ace wanted to cheer. Instead, he ducked around, biting off a rant about where the hell the network had been when she was kidnapped in Mexico.

Honey and Leroy came to them, walked beside. "You okay, Kitty?"

Kitty nodded at Honey, but didn't stop. "I need to go home. I'm sorry. Ace, please."

He'd never seen her so scared, barring that night in the hallway.

"No worries, darlin'." He gave Leroy what he hoped was a rueful smile. "Why don't y'all have a few days together and then come see us up to the ranch?"

Leroy nodded. "Maybe a week or two. I got some plans for my woman."

"I hear you." He winked, and they all stopped in-between the two sets of glass doors between the charter area and the rest of the airport to give hugs and such. "We're just gonna go on, then. Steele can get us a rental, yeah?"

Cash held up his phone. "Got two waiting. Me and Steele are heading to Omaha for the event."

God, he had amazing friends. "Thanks, y'all. Get us to the rental counter and I'll cut you loose."

"I'll tell 'em you're on medical leave. Want four or six weeks?"

"Six." He didn't even hesitate. Kitty was pregnant and freaked out. He needed time.

"You got it." Cash smiled at Kitty. "I'm glad to meet you, sweetheart. You holler when you're ready, we'll all celebrate knowing you."

Kitty stopped and kissed Cash's cheek. "Thank you."

Cash patted her shoulder awkwardly, then punched Ace on the arm. "Later, buddy."

"See you. Keep Steele out of trouble."

Ace signed for the rental and got Kitty into it, avoiding the damned media who were everywhere. Kitty never said a word, just let him do.

He got them headed out of Houston before he glanced over again. She was so pale, so quiet. "You want that chocolate we got?"

She looked over at him, shook her head. "No. I want a strawberry milkshake from McDonalds when we stop, though." One hand reached out for him. "It's real, right? We're really going home?"

"To the ranch? We are." He took her hand. He was good—they had an automatic.

"Okay. I want that. To go home, I mean." She held on tight, and it wasn't long before the tears came, a hard, fierce storm.

If he could have stopped, he would have, but they were in the teeth of rush hour traffic. He couldn't stop for nearly half an hour, and by then, the storm had passed.

It was probably just as well. She seemed glad he'd let it go. "Will Whataburger work? They have incredible shakes."

"That sounds perfect." She stretched a little, nodded. "In fact, I might even have a little burger, too."

Oh, thank God.

"I might have a big one." He could eat a whole fucking cow at this point, although Lucky had fed them eggs and bacon and toast kind of hysterically.

"You can have two and share your French fries with me."

"Oh, we can do better than that." If nothing else he'd get her to eat Texas toast. She had an unnatural fondness for it.

Her fingers squeezed his, then her head rested on his shoulder.

That was it. She was relaxing. "Need to stop and hit the bathroom, darlin', or you want drive-through?"

"Let's just drive through. I want to shower, sleep in your bed with you."

He wrapped his fingers around hers tighter. "Yes, please. We can go swimming in the morning."

"That sounds perfect. We need to call your mom, too. Tell her you're safe."

Shit, he needed to tell her more than that.

She was going to have a preacher at the house by tomorrow afternoon once she found out about the baby. Not that Ace minded. Cash and Steele were already calling her his wife.

And God knew Ace wasn't letting her go, ever again.

What he was gonna do was get her shake and some food and get her where she felt safe.

Then he was taking her to a doctor, making sure she was healthy, then he was going to make her legal.

Damn it.

They went through the drive-through and Kitty ate some of her toast, a few fries and her whole shake. At which point she passed out cold.

Ace poked her a couple times, just to be sure she was asleep but not dead. Then he called his momma.

"Baby boy. Tell me you're safe."

"Hey, Momma. I'm fine. I got Kitty, and she's okay."

"Oh, praise Jesus. Are you coming home?"

"We are. She's..." He glanced at Kitty. "She's pregnant."

"I... It's... They didn't hurt. I mean, son, is it yours?"

Ace laughed. That was the one thing he'd never doubted. "It is. She tried to tell me before she left. I was kinda mean."

"Oh. Well, it happens. She's okay? I can call the preacher and Dr. Foster in the morning."

"She is. She's a little bruised." The preacher would have to wait a little.

"Oh, good lord. I'll put some food in the kitchen, run out tomorrow and buy her some clothes and stuff. Poor baby girl."

"She's tough, but this was harsh. I'd love for you bring her some soft stuff to wear and maybe a nice bathing suit, huh?"

"Okay, I'll run to the Wal-Mart right now. A baby, huh? You tickled, son?" He heard the unspoken 'are you okay' right in there.

"I am. I was so worried, but we got it under control now."

"I'll make sure Doc sees her ASAP. You...you took care of shit, yeah? He won't be coming for her?"

"I took care of it, Momma. Me and Steele and Cash. It's okay."

"Good boy." She sighed. "I like her. She makes you smile. I love you, baby. You be careful."

"I will. Thanks, Momma. Oh, could you get ice cream?" Kitty would eat that, he'd bet.

"What flavor?"

"Strawberry. That one that starts with an H."

"You got it. Does she drink juice or fizzy water or only tea?"

"She likes water and tea and apple juice." He was proud that he knew this stuff.

"Okay. You want Bud Lite?"

"I do. A case. Steele will be down after the next two events are done."

"Good deal. Love you, son. Kiss Kitty for me and tell her I'll see her late-late tomorrow."

"I will, Momma. Thank you for everything."

"Anything." He heard a sound suspiciously like a sob. "I'm going to be a granny, huh?"

He chuckled. "Didn't think it would happen?"

"I knew it would. You're a cowboy. But it didn't think it would be so soon."

"Very soon. Love you."

"Love you, baby boy. Drive safe."

She hung up and he glanced down at his girl, who was still leaning, still sound asleep.

Bless her heart. She had to have been terrified to sleep.

He didn't look at the bruises, because that would just make him mad.

He'd take her home, clean her up, and love on her.

Then he'd make sure she never got into trouble like that again.

Chapter Twenty

Kitty sat by the pool in the bright pink swimsuit Carol had bought for her. Ace was out doing something with the animals and the cowboys, and she was resting. Sunning.

She thought Ace was maybe scared of her a little bit. After all, she'd been back for two days and he hadn't really touched her.

Maybe the whole bruised, choked, almost thick middle thing was intimidating.

Still, it gave her time to catch up on her reading. Ace had three new thrillers and his momma had brought romances. There was ice cream. They were going to the doctor's tomorrow, to make sure that Peanut was okay. She knew it was, though. It had to be. The kid was tough like its daddy. Right?

She slipped into the pool, needing to cool off. Late September was brutally hot, somehow, like Texas didn't know it was autumn. *Oh, much better.* Ace had set up a couple of umbrellas to give the pool a little shade at the ends. Nice.

She started swimming, going from one end to the other.

Her hands cut through the water slowly, making her feel lazy and kind of dreamy.

She turned over, closed her eyes, and floated.

"Hey, darlin'." When she opened her eyes, Ace stood by the pool, smiling down at her.

"Hey." Her heart sped up and she headed for the edge. "How're you?"

"Not bad. You look pretty comfy in there." He tilted his hat back a little, those dimples flashing.

"I was dozing, cooling off." She chuckled. "Being lazy."

"Nothing lazy about it." Ace started stripping down, taking off his shirt and boots. He made her mouth dry — tight, compact. Firm.

Kitty bit her bottom lip, watched every second. He had a ripped little belly, hard-muscled arms, and when he pushed down his pants, a tight ass and great legs.

"Ace." God, she wanted him.

"Oh, thank God." He struck a pose wearing his hat and a growing hard-on. It was hilarious and endearing.

She reached out for him. "Either come down and touch me or help me up."

"I'll come there. It's cooler." His grin widened and he tossed his hat off to one side before sliding into the water. His hands landed on her waist and she almost moaned.

Her nipples went hard from that single touch.

"So pretty. Been so worried about you, darlin'." He kissed her cheek, her mouth, her chin. He wasn't afraid to touch her now.

"I need you, Ace." It was simple, bald, but true. She needed him to love her.

"I need you, too, Kitty. I been waiting, wanting to make sure you were okay, but I think I'm done with that." He lifted her a little, going to the steps of the pool and sinking down with her on top.

"I won't be okay until you touch me." She leaned down, took the kiss that she'd dreamed about, let her cowboy know how badly she needed to feel like she was truly home.

Ace kissed her as if he was starving for her, like he'd used up every bit of gentle he had.

He eased her swimsuit straps down, freed her breasts. His hands found them almost immediately, cupping her. She felt it, the line of need going straight to her clit.

He rubbed her nipples, his pelvis bucking up, his cock hard against her. Hooray for that. She'd been worried.

Her thoughts scattered, the touch of his hands enough to make her whimper.

He pushed at her, pulled, his mouth moving on her skin, too. Her throat, her shoulder.

She nodded, letting him touch all those marks, make them his.

Ace went over every one. He was clearly on a mission.

"Ace." She arched, leaned back over his arms, her breasts arcing up over the water.

"Sweet." He took one nipple in his mouth, sucking hard.

A filthy word burst out of her, her fingers on his head as her hips rolled. So big. A shot of pure need slammed along her spine.

"Need inside you, darlin'."

"Please. Please, now." She shoved the rest of the suit off, let it float away.

"Yes." He lifted her, his legs spreading hers, then brought her down, his erection pressing between her legs.

"Oh, God. Ace." Her eyes felt like they were rolling, her body ached.

"Yeah." He eased inside her, his thick cock hotter than anything.

She'd never needed so much, not even the first time. His hands were on her hips, helping her move.

"Kitty." He moaned her name against her lips, driving her, driving both of them.

"Love." She whispered the word, meaning it.

His eyes opened wide, his gaze fixed to hers. "Oh, fuck."

His body bucked, his grip tight enough to leave bruises of his own.

She nodded. "I do. Love you. Harder."

"Yes." He moved faster, slamming into her, pulling her down to meet him. "Kitty…"

Her entire body shuddered, shook, the need inside her bigger than anything she'd ever felt.

He curled in close, his lips next to her ear. "I love you, darlin'."

She cried out, her entire world taken over by her orgasm.

Ace convulsed against her, his cry ringing out.

She held on tight, her body shaking with the aftershocks.

He cradled her against his chest, keeping her from floating away. He kissed her cheek, right by her ear, making her shiver.

"Oh." She closed her eyes, breathed. She could stay right here. Forever.

"I'm glad you're home, darlin'."

"I knew you'd come for me." *Home.*

"I had to." He chuckled. "I was going to soon, anyway, but then Honey called."

"She and Leroy have a signal. They were going to let him leave, but he said no." Leroy was her best friend, and she had no doubt that he'd saved her life.

"Good on him. I owe him."

"I owe you my life."

Ace pulled back enough to look at her. "Well, I'll keep it, if you want me to."

Kitty's heart stopped and she searched his eyes, hoping he meant what she thought he did. "It's yours."

"Good." Ace nodded, never looking away. "I don't feel trapped. I want you to know that upfront."

"I wanted to tell you before I left, but I didn't want to do it over the phone. I found out that day."

"I know." Sighing, he hugged her tightly, pulling them out of the water a little. "I figured it out when Honey told me."

She leaned back. "You knew before I told you?"

Turkey.

That got her a crookedy grin. "Honey said. I figured that was why you were so weird when we talked. I was pissed at everyone."

"Yeah. I was scared." She touched his smile, traced it.

"Well, promise me you won't ever run off and get kidnapped again because you're scared, okay?"

She arched an eyebrow. "I went to Mexico for work."

"You ran off and got kidnapped." He nodded, like they were the same thing.

She pushed off him, shook her head. "I was working, Ace. It's what I do. I'm a reporter."

Where is that damn swimsuit?

Ace held it out to her as if he knew she needed to cover up. "I know that, darlin'. Having a baby changes some things."

"Thank you." She tried to figure out if she could tug it on. "I didn't run off."

"Here, darlin'." Ace got his shirt and put it around her, leading her to sit in the lounge chair by the pool. "I'm not accusing you of anything, okay? I was scared as hell and I know you love your job, but it makes me crazy and I try not to be an ass."

"I was scared, too, but I had to go." She curled up in his shirt.

"Can we talk about it next time, before you go off?" He sat next to her, hand on her leg.

"We'll have to, won't we?" She touched his fingers, slow and careful. "At some point, we'll have a baby to take care of."

"That we will." That had him smiling again. "A little cowboy."

"A little peanut." She winked.

"Peanut, huh? I like it." Ace kissed her, then leaned.

She closed her eyes, listened to the silence.

"You want some sun lotion, darlin'? Or just to go in and have a nap with me?"

She met his eyes, found him a smile. "I could nap."

"Me, too." Naked as the day he was born, Ace stood and helped her up.

She let him tuck her into his side, take her inside. Let him curl her close, one hand on her belly while they slept.

* * * *

Ace couldn't stop grinning. They'd been to the doctor — not Doc Madding. The man wasn't much for birthing and all. The doc said the baby was perfect, though.

That was damned important.

His momma was waiting to take him and Kitty to lunch, and he steered Kitty out to meet Momma with a hand on her waist.

He'd remember that odd rushing sound the rest of his life.

His baby.

Goddamn.

They'd done that ultrasound thing, but he hadn't really been able to make anything out.

Still. It was a baby with a heartbeat and at least one arm.

A huge arm, like some horror movie thing. It was hilarious.

Momma came trotting up, holding a couple of bags from the CVS. "Well?"

Kitty offered her a tentative smile. "It looks like a baby. Strong heartbeat. It's still little bitty."

Momma shrugged. "Y'all ain't big. She'll be wee."

"She, huh?" He shook his head. "Why she?"

"A granny knows." She handed Kitty a bottle of apple juice. "What do you want to eat, baby girl?"

Kitty blinked. God, that was cute. Momma'd decided that Kitty was family—bringing food and clothes, fussing over her.

"I'm not terribly hungry."

"Nonsense. You've just been stressed."

"That's what I've been telling her."

Kitty looked at him but Momma hooted. "I am dying for pancakes. Let's go to Ruby's."

"Sounds like a plan." Ruby's puffy waffle might entice Kitty to pig out.

Kitty stayed close, drank her juice. She was still quiet, weirdly still.

Ace hugged her close with the arm around her. "You okay, darlin'?"

"I am. I just…I was worried. About the baby being— you know. Hurt."

"Well, now you know better, huh? I mean, he's Hellboy, but…" He kissed her forehead, real gentle-like.

"I do." Her eyes got a little wet and her fingers twisted with his.

Ace hoped to hell that was good crying. He could never tell the damned difference, but every woman he knew said that there was a difference.

Momma caught his eye, winked. "Do you like blueberry pancakes, Kitty?"

Kitty smiled, nodded. "I'm not a picky eater, Carol."

"Oh, good to know. I love pancakes." Momma chattered on, leading them toward the diner.

By the time they were settled in with two coffees and another apple juice, Kitty's color was back.

Ace smiled at her, his hand automatically reaching for hers.

"So, are y'all going to stay at the ranch? Have you talked about which room the nursery's going to be?" Momma loved to decorate.

"No, ma'am." He saw Momma's face fall and he shook his head. "I mean yes, we're staying at the ranch. No, we haven't settled on a room."

"Oh. Oh, God. Y'all. I damn near had a heart attack." She patted Kitty's hand. "I promise not to be a meddling mother-in-law, but I am going to granny y'all's babies and that would be hard in New York City."

Kitty teared up a little again and Ace took a deep breath. "Let the girl eat before we got to make big plans, Momma."

Momma kicked him under the table, but nodded. "It's okay, baby girl. I promise. Pregnant women cry and you've had a time of it."

Kitty gave her a watery smile. "I'm just tired."

"Have you called your momma?"

Kitty shook her head. "My folks aren't interested. I... They're very... They don't believe that women ought to leave home before marriage. They don't want me."

Momma got that pursed-lip look that said she was building up to a mad-on. "Well, then. That's their loss."

"Honey and Leroy know. That's Kitty's family, Momma."

"Still, how could anyone not want her?" Momma glared at him, then grinned. "Of course, I suppose you're grateful no other boy caught her, aren't you?"

"Hell, yes." He gave Kitty a slow smile, his fingers rubbing up on hers.

That earned him a blush and Kitty relaxed and leaned in a little. "I never thought I'd know someone like Ace."

"He's one of a kind, huh?"

Ace didn't roll his eyes, but he wanted to. He was just a cowboy. Nothing special.

"He's exactly what I need."

"Awesome." Momma clapped her hands.

His heart did a little double bump. God, he had it bad.

He'd told her, though, right? So he could be a dork now.

Momma ordered pancakes and Kitty ordered the Belgian waffle, which made Momma smile.

Ace ordered the special. Pancakes with strawberries, eggs, bacon, sausage... Nerves.

"So, when are you going to get married? And don't tell me you're not, because I'll beat you both."

Ace glanced at Kitty. "We haven't had a chance to talk on it, Momma." He wanted to ask, damn it, not settle it at the kitchen table.

Kitty looked over at Momma, smiled a little. "Are you sure you want him to ask me? I might be a screaming harpy."

Momma's laugh filled the restaurant, merry and tickled.

"She knows better." Ace had told Momma all about Kitty. Everything up until the last few weeks.

"I was thinking about the planning, the people." Momma shrugged and lowered her voice. "The dress. Honey, you're tiny. You're gonna show early."

"I don't want anything big." Kitty shook her head, lips tight. "Nothing busy."

Ace laughed a little, shaking his head. "I might make her wear jeans."

Her ass looked amazing in denim, especially with heels on. Could she wear heels now?

Momma nodded. "Nothing big, then. Me and Steele and Cash, your Honey and Leroy. Lucky if he'll come. Just family. Everybody in jeans." Momma's eyes landed on Kitty again. "No black."

Kitty blinked, then laughed. "I'll have to shop."

She would look amazing in pink. Baby pink. He wanted white for the wedding, though. A white shirt.

"Now, honey. That is something I'm made for." Momma hooted, beamed at her. "We should go to Dallas."

Kitty's shoulders went up around her ears, her smile fading.

"Maybe we should wait on that, Momma." He gave his momma a warning glance.

Momma glanced at Kitty, sighed softly and nodded.

"Anyway, as soon as Kitty gets some rest we'll start making plans. We'll get you and Honey together, huh?"

"Of course." She met Kitty's eyes again. "I'm excited, honey. Forgive me?"

"There's nothing to forgive. I'm just..." Kitty shook her head, fluttered a little. "I don't want to see people right now. Not so many people."

"Well, then, we won't." Momma brightened. "I bet you know how to shop online!"

There was that smile. "Yeah. Yeah, in fact, I'm sort of a champion."

"Well, there you go." Ace gave his momma a pat on the knee under the table. Thank goodness for her.

The food came and Kitty turned a little green, seemed a little panicked. Momma looked at her, nodded. "Take one bite, baby girl. It'll stop."

"Yeah?"

"I swear."

Kitty's hand was shaking but she got that one bite in her and in a few seconds her color came back. "Oh."

Better. Ace watched her real careful-like for the next few bites.

Momma beamed but didn't say a thing, just set to her own food. Kitty started eating then as if she was starving, the strawberries disappearing. He reckoned they needed a flat of those at the ranch.

Maybe two. Ace dug in finally, no longer worried that she'd fall over.

Soon Momma had her laughing, had her making plans for the baby's room. Through the whole meal, one of her hands was on his thigh, like she needed to make sure he was right there.

He held on when he could, smiled for her every time she glanced over, and was just damned happy. He needed to hunt a ring.

Something unusual, something interesting.

His girl needed something better than the same old thing.

He'd put his head together with Lucky, maybe, if he could get ahold of the fool man. Lucky had been married.

Kitty reached over, touched his lips. "You okay, Ace?"

"Hmm?" He kissed her fingertips. "I am. I'm better than that, actually."

"Awesome." She pinked a little, but her smile was big. "You were thinking very deep thoughts."

Momma murmured something, got up and headed to the counter to talk to the hostess.

"I was thinking about what kind of ring to get you." Lord. His mouth was on autopilot.

Kitty grinned. "Were you? What kind?"

"Something different." He studied her a moment. "Maybe a ruby in a real simple setting. You can have diamonds on the actual band. Little ones. Nothing gaudy."

Listen to him, talking out his ass.

"Oh…" God, no woman had never looked at him like she did. Not one. "That sounds beautiful. What about you?"

Momma sat back down. "I have his daddy's ring, if you wouldn't mind, Kitty."

"Oh, that would be perfect."

Ace blinked a little, feeling a tiny bit overwhelmed. "I — thank you."

Momma just nodded. "No one deserves it like you."

"Well, I sure appreciate it." He missed his dad fierce.

Momma grabbed his hand, squeezed.

Damn, they were all a little watery now.

"Okay. Let's go shopping." Momma grinned. "Just one little baby outfit, huh? In green or yellow."

"What do you say, darlin'?"

"I like yellow."

Ace nodded, finishing up his last bite of food. "Then let's do it."

Momma beamed, took Kitty's hand. "Ace can get the bill. There's the cutest little store, just across the street…"

"I got it." He laughed, patting Kitty's hand. "Go on, darlin'. I'll be right there."

Kitty kissed his cheek. "Love you. See you in a few."

Just as casual and easy as you please.

"Love you, too," he murmured, and watched her walk off with his momma. God, he did. Love her.

Now, about that ring…

Chapter Twenty-One

Kitty sat at the computer, staring at the American Airlines website.

She needed to go to the city, deal with her apartment, deal with things. She needed to do this, to be strong and go talk to the network, figure out what her position was going to be.

Especially since she was going to be doing it without Leroy.

The man had called her this morning, let her know that the NBC affiliate in Houston had picked him up, given him a job where he'd be home every night.

Ace hadn't asked her about her job or her apartment or anything. He'd been very gentle with the real life stuff, letting her be a big girl.

She wrapped her arms around her middle, holding herself. She'd been in worse scrapes. She had. She had to... God, she didn't want to deal. She wanted to hide and be hormonal and let Ace handle shit.

Her phone rang and she grabbed it. "Hello?"

"Katherine? It's Tom. It's been a while. I wanted you to know we've found you a new cameraman. We need you in here on Monday, okay? We've got an Afghan military leader that's interested in an exclusive, but he wants you."

* * * *

Ace pulled off his jeans and boots and grabbed swim trunks before heading to the office to find Kitty.

He heard her crying before he got all the way down the hall, then the sound of violent retching.

Shit. Ace flew into the bathroom off the office, going to his knees next to her. "Darlin'? Are you okay?"

She shook her head. "No. No! The network called me! They want me to go again, with somebody else."

"Who? What are you talking about?" She was so not going back to Mexico. Not without Leroy. No way.

She sat there, drenched with sweat. Ace stood and got her a glass of cold water and she took it, hands shaking as she started the water, rinsed her mouth. "The network. There's a man in Afghanistan. They want me in New York by Monday."

"Afghanistan."

No. God, no. No fucking way was he letting his girl and their baby go into a goddamn war zone. Shit, she couldn't even handle the damned Wal-Mart without him right there.

Kitty nodded then shook her head, tears streaking her cheeks. "They say I don't have a choice."

"Bullshit." She had all the choices in the world. "Tell them to stuff it. Hell, I'll tell them."

Her eyes went wide and Ace thought he saw a little bit of hope in them. Something he hadn't expected since he knew he was on his high horse. "Oh, that'll go over great. Hey, Tom, we talked about it and I'm not going."

"You know it." He nodded, pulling her into his arms. "Honey texted me, so I know about Leroy. You tell them you have a whole different life now."

"I don't want to go." She started crying again, holding on tight. "I want to stay home and paint Peanut's room and eat strawberries."

Secretly, Ace thought pregnancy hormones made women a little crazy. Still, Momma said it was normal and that he could cope with it and keep feeding her. Kitty said she'd get big as a house, but that was bullshit, too. She was starting to show a little was all.

"They won't let me come back, I don't think, if I drop this."

"So, don't go back." He pulled her to her feet, helping her wash up while he tried to find how to say what came next. "Darlin', the Mexico story made you gold. You can tell them to go to hell and work for anyone. Or you can do your own thing. Hell, you can take a year off, be a woman of mystery, and still be hot when you come back."

"You don't think I'm a coward?"

A coward. Jesus. Tilting her chin up, Ace met her eyes with his. He could be a chauvinist pig but she made him so proud, because she was fierce. "I think you're the bravest lady I know."

"I just... I thought I was going to be an anchor but..." She stopped short, blinked, then looked at him, a little stunned. Before he could ask her what was up, she had his hand on her belly, the tiniest little hiccup of her muscles under his fingers.

Ace melted a little, his eyes stinging. "Oh, Kitty. Feel that."

She nodded, looking at him in pure shock. "It's... Wow."

Yeah, and she wasn't going to Afghanistan. Not now. She needed him and home and peace. Not to mention that there was still no fucking way he was letting his wife and baby go to a goddamn war zone. *No way.*

That weird little fluttering thing happened again and Kitty gasped. "Can you feel that?"

"I can." Lord. That was their Peanut. Theirs. He leaned down, kissed her lips, fingers splayed on that sweet belly.

I got you, baby. I ain't letting nothing bad happen to you, ever.

"I want you to call them, Kitty. Please? Tell them to fuck off. You have a place here, until the day you die. You don't have to go."

She searched his eyes, lip quivering. "I never thought I'd do this. But I want to. No more petty tyrants."

"It's okay, though, right?" It had to be. He'd always known he wanted to settle down, have kids.

Her little nod made the pit of his belly ache. "You're my true north, Ace."

"Darlin'." He kissed her, because what else could he do?

Well, that and hand her the phone so she could tell those Yankees to stuff their job so they could call the preacher.

About the Author

Texan to the bone and an unrepentant Daddy's Girl, BA spends her days with her basset hounds, getting tattooed, texting her sisters, and eating Mexican food. When she's not doing that, she's writing. She spends her days off watching rodeo, knitting and surfing Pinterest in the name of research. BA's personal saviors include her wife, Julia, her best friend, Sean, and coffee. Lots of good coffee.

BA Tortuga loves to hear from readers. You can find her contact information, website and author biography at http://www.totallybound.com

Home of Erotic Romance